ANN M. MARTIN

THE BABY-SITTERS CLUB

THE TRUTH ABOUT STACEY

A GRAPHIC NOVEL BY
RAINA TELGEMEIER
WITH COLOR BY BRADEN LAMB

An Imprint of
SCHOLASTIC

KRISTY THOMAS
PRESIDENT

CLAUDIA KISHI
VICE PRESIDENT

MARY ANNE SPIER
SECRETARY

STACEY MCGILL
TREASURER

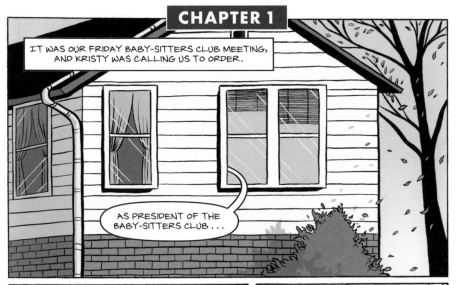

CHAPTER 1

IT WAS OUR FRIDAY BABY-SITTERS CLUB MEETING, AND KRISTY WAS CALLING US TO ORDER.

AS PRESIDENT OF THE BABY-SITTERS CLUB . . .

. . . I HEREBY MOVE THAT WE FIGURE OUT WHAT TO DO WHEN MRS. NEWTON GOES TO THE HOSPITAL TO HAVE HER BABY.

WHAT DO YOU MEAN?

MR. AND MRS. NEWTON WILL NEED SOMEONE TO TAKE CARE OF JAMIE, WHENEVER IT HAPPENS. SMART BABY-SITTERS WOULD BE READY FOR THE OCCASION.

I THINK THAT'S A GOOD IDEA, KRISTY.

MAYBE FROM NOW ON, ONE OF US SHOULD BE FREE EACH AFTERNOON, SO MRS. NEWTON WILL BE GUARANTEED A SITTER.

THAT SEEMS LIKE A WASTE.... BABIES CAN BE LATE. TWO OR THREE **WEEKS** LATE.

CLAUDIA'S RIGHT.... WE COULD BE GIVING UP A LOT OF PERFECTLY GOOD AFTERNOONS FOR NOTHING.

MY NAME'S STACEY MCGILL.

I JUST MOVED TO THIS TEENY-WEENY TOWN, STONEYBROOK, CONNECTICUT. WHICH IS QUITE A SHOCK, SINCE I GREW UP IN . . .

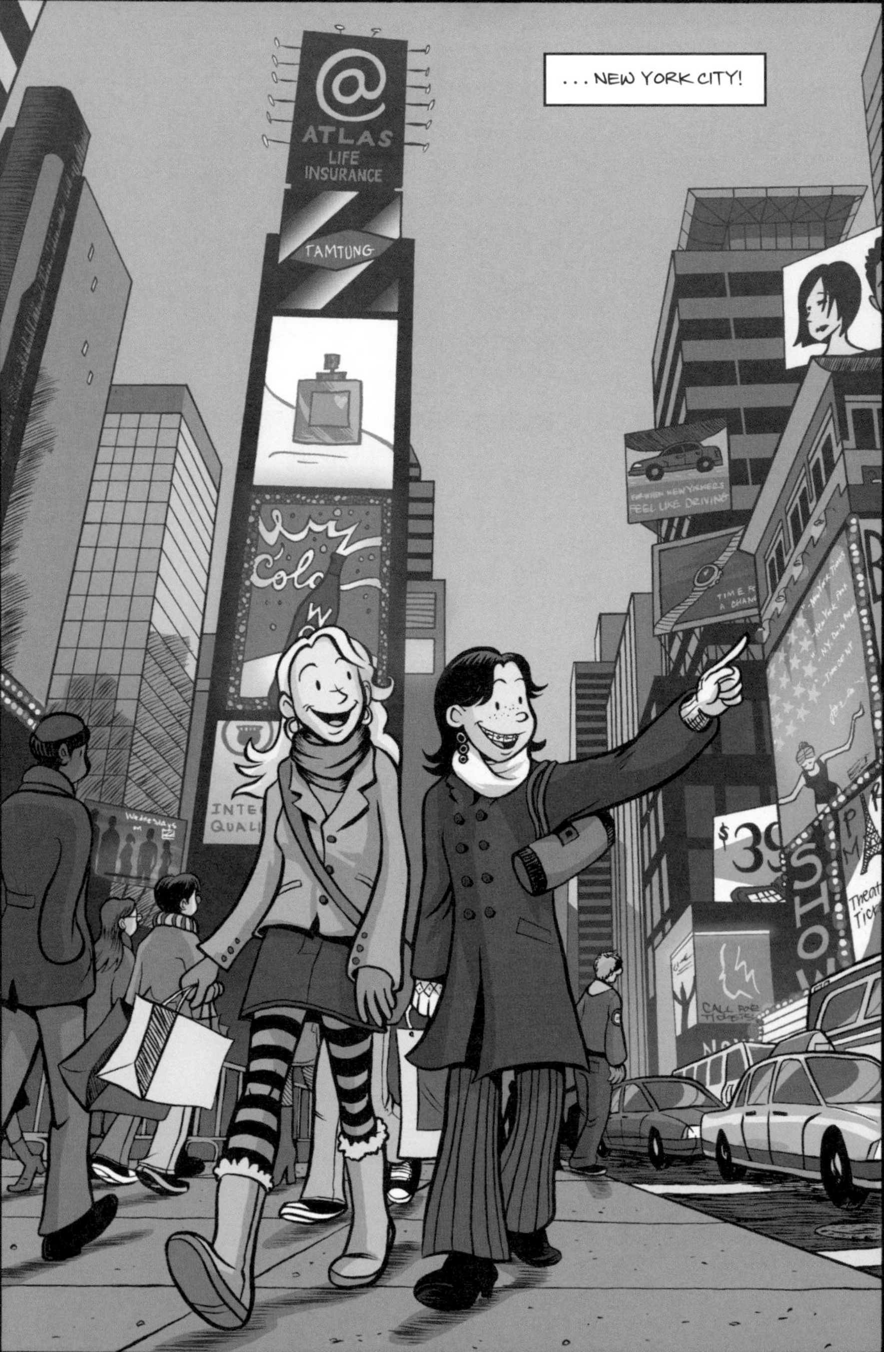
. . . NEW YORK CITY!
ATLAS
LIFE
INSURANCE
TAMTUNG
FEEL LIKE DRIVING
SHOW
CALL FOR
TICKETS

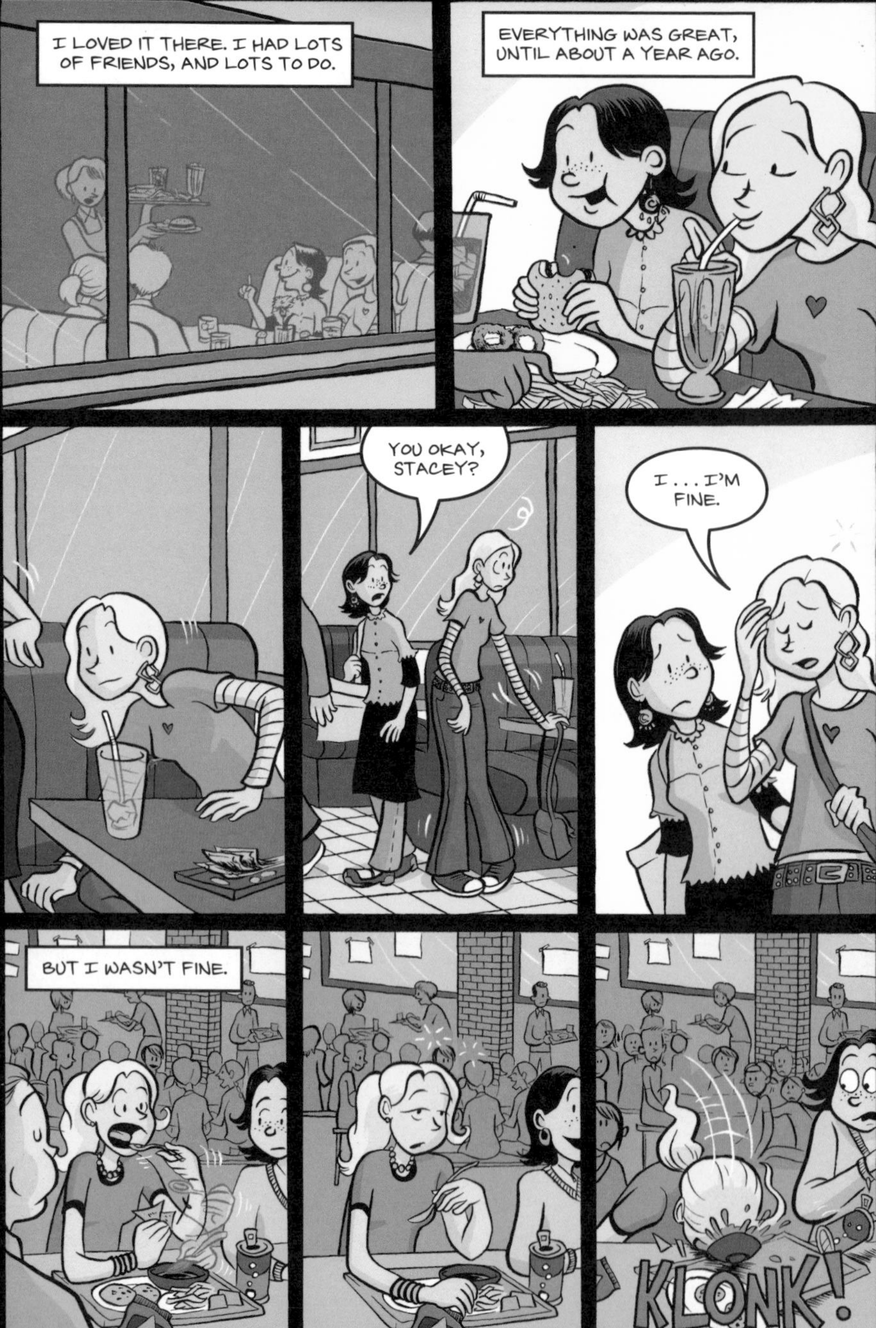
I LOVED IT THERE. I HAD LOTS OF FRIENDS, AND LOTS TO DO.
EVERYTHING WAS GREAT, UNTIL ABOUT A YEAR AGO.
YOU OKAY, STACEY?
I . . . I'M FINE.
BUT I WASN'T FINE.
KLONK!

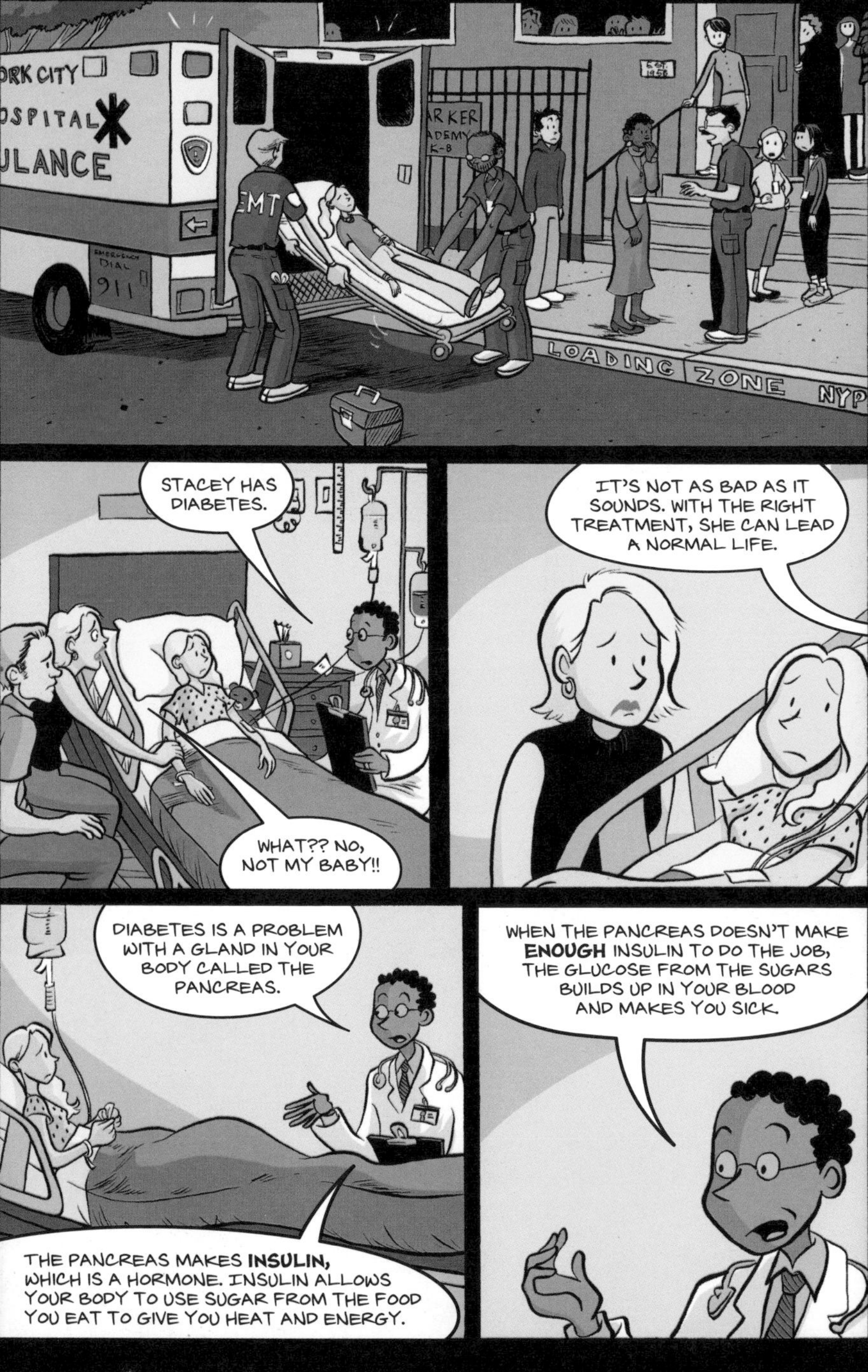
ORK CITY
OSPITAL
ULANCE
EMT
EMERGENCY DIAL 911
ARKER
ADEMY
K-8
LOADING ZONE NYP
STACEY HAS DIABETES.
WHAT?? NO, NOT MY BABY!!
IT'S NOT AS BAD AS IT SOUNDS. WITH THE RIGHT TREATMENT, SHE CAN LEAD A NORMAL LIFE.
DIABETES IS A PROBLEM WITH A GLAND IN YOUR BODY CALLED THE PANCREAS.
THE PANCREAS MAKES **INSULIN,** WHICH IS A HORMONE. INSULIN ALLOWS YOUR BODY TO USE SUGAR FROM THE FOOD YOU EAT TO GIVE YOU HEAT AND ENERGY.
WHEN THE PANCREAS DOESN'T MAKE **ENOUGH** INSULIN TO DO THE JOB, THE GLUCOSE FROM THE SUGARS BUILDS UP IN YOUR BLOOD AND MAKES YOU SICK.

BUT, IF YOU EAT A HEALTHY DIET, AND GIVE YOURSELF INSULIN INJECTIONS EVERY DAY--

WHAT?!

SO THE NEXT THING I KNEW, I WAS LEARNING TO GIVE MYSELF INSULIN SHOTS. I DID START TO FEEL BETTER PRETTY QUICKLY.

DOCTOR, ARE YOU SURE SHE CAN DO THIS ALL BY HERSELF?

MOM!!

AND OVERNIGHT, MOM AND DAD TURNED INTO THE WORLD'S MOST OVERPROTECTIVE PARENTS.

HONEY, YOU'RE STILL LOSING WEIGHT.

I WONDER IF YOU'RE EATING ENOUGH? I DON'T KNOW IF THIS NEW DIET SOUNDS RIGHT.

DIABETIC DIETS
CARB SUGAR

I'VE MADE YOU AN APPOINTMENT WITH ANOTHER DOCTOR ON TUESDAY, JUST TO SEE IF--

MOMMMM!!

BUT THAT WASN'T THE WORST PART.

LAINE! IT'S SO GOOD TO SEE YOU AGAIN! HOW'S SCHOOL BEEN? I WAS AFRAID I'D...

UH, GOTTA GO, STACE . . . SEE YA.

MY BEST FRIEND, LAINE, STOPPED TALKING TO ME. SHE NEVER EVEN TRIED TO FIND OUT WHAT WAS WRONG.... WAS SHE SCARED OF ME?

HI, MRS. CUMMINGS... IT'S STACEY. IS LAINE HOME?

I'M SORRY, STACEY.... SHE CAN'T COME TO THE PHONE RIGHT NOW.

No!

SINCE LAINE WAS OUR LEADER, EVERYONE ELSE PRETTY MUCH FOLLOWED HER EXAMPLE. I FOUND MYSELF ALONE NEARLY ALL THE TIME.

I DIDN'T FEEL AT HOME ANYMORE.

SO WHEN MOM AND DAD ANNOUNCED WE WERE MOVING AWAY...

...I DIDN'T EVEN CARE.

I DIDN'T MAKE A SINGLE NEW FRIEND HERE IN STONEYBROOK UNTIL I MET CLAUDIA. SOON AFTER, SHE INVITED ME TO BE A MEMBER OF THE BABY-SITTERS CLUB, AND THINGS BEGAN TO LOOK UP.

...AND WHAT ABOUT A NIGHTTIME PLAN?

YEAH, **LOTS** OF BABIES ARE BORN IN THE MIDDLE OF THE NIGHT.

RING!

CLAUDIA, KRISTY, AND MARY ANNE HAVE QUICKLY BECOME MY NEW BEST FRIENDS, AND OUR CLUB HAS BEEN A HUGE SUCCESS! WE SIT FOR TONS OF THE KIDS IN OUR NEIGHBORHOOD.

WELL, WE'LL FIGURE SOMETHING OUT. . . . WHO WANTS CANDY?

BABY-SITTERS CLUB, STACEY SPEAKING.

HI, DR. JOHANSSEN! . . . MONDAY? WE'LL CALL YOU RIGHT BACK.

MAYBE WE COULD CALL MRS. NEWTON AND ASK HER IF--

CLAUDIA! CLAUDIA!!

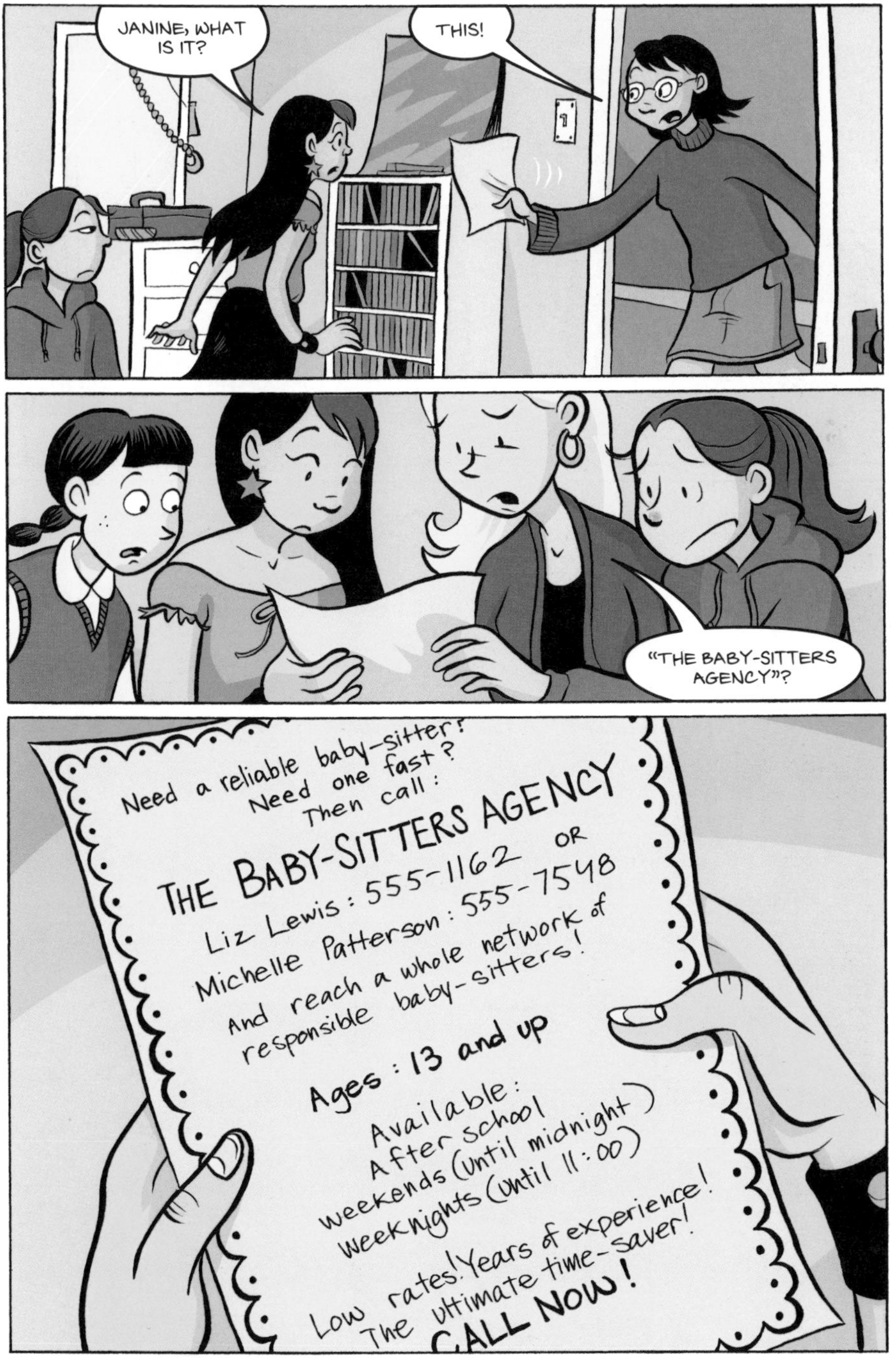
JANINE, WHAT IS IT?
THIS!
"THE BABY-SITTERS AGENCY"?
Need a reliable baby-sitter? Need one fast? Then call:
THE BABY-SITTERS AGENCY
Liz Lewis: 555-1162 OR
Michelle Patterson: 555-7548
And reach a whole network of responsible baby-sitters!
Ages: 13 and up
Available:
After school
weekends (until midnight)
weeknights (until 11:00)
Low rates! Years of experience!
The ultimate time-saver!
CALL NOW!

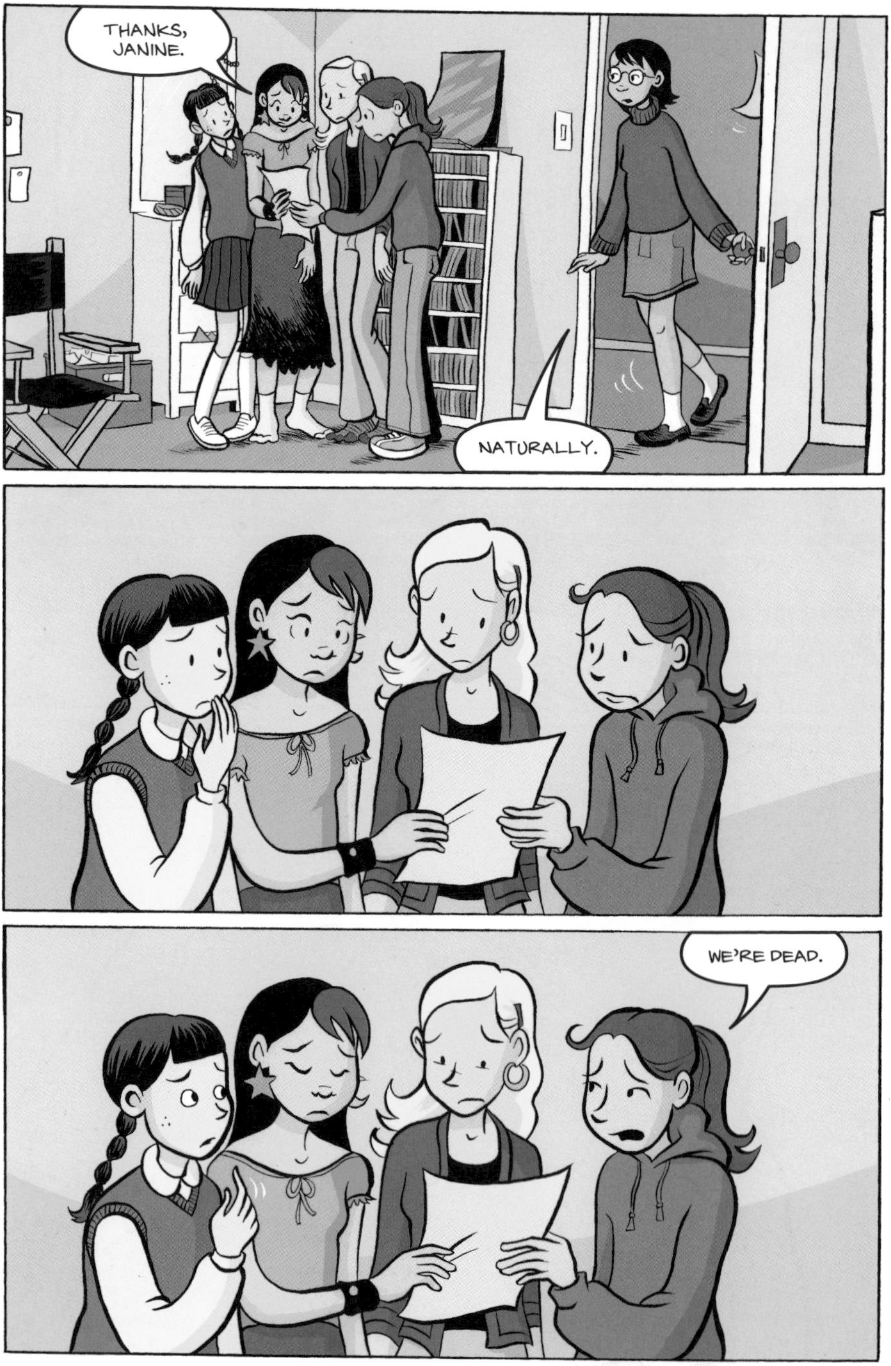
THANKS, JANINE.
NATURALLY.
WE'RE DEAD.

CHAPTER 2

A FEW MINUTES LATER...

THE OTHER BABY-SITTERS ARE OLDER THAN WE ARE. THEY CAN STAY OUT LATER....

WHO **ARE** LIZ LEWIS AND MICHELLE PATTERSON?

THE FLIER SAYS THE BABY-SITTERS ARE "THIRTEEN AND OLDER." LIZ AND MICHELLE PROBABLY GO TO THE HIGH SCHOOL.... I WONDER IF MY BROTHERS KNOW THEM?

NO, THEY GO TO STONEYBROOK MIDDLE SCHOOL. THEY'RE EIGHTH GRADERS.

RRRIP

ARE YOU FRIENDS WITH THEM, CLAUD?

I'D NEVER BE FRIENDS WITH GIRLS LIKE THEM. LIFESAVER?

UM, MY DIABETES? I CAN'T HAVE ONE.

OH, YEAH. SORRY, STACEY. --KRISTY?

IT'S OKAY.

SO WHAT'S WRONG WITH THEM?

THEY HAVE SMART MOUTHS, THEY SASS THE TEACHERS, THEY HANG AROUND AT THE MALL. Y'KNOW, **THAT** KIND OF KID.

IT DOESN'T MEAN THEY'RE NOT GOOD BABY-SITTERS. . . .

I'D BE SURPRISED IF THEY WERE.

I WONDER HOW THE AGENCY WORKS. THERE'S ONLY TWO NAMES ON THIS FLIER, BUT IT SAYS YOU CAN GET IN TOUCH WITH A "WHOLE NETWORK OF RESPONSIBLE BABY-SITTERS."

LIZ AND MICHELLE KNOW HOW TO GO AFTER CUSTOMERS. THIS FLIER IS A LOT BETTER THAN OURS WAS.

HEY! I HAVE AN IDEA.

LET'S CALL THE AGENCY AND PRETEND WE NEED A SITTER, THEN CALL BACK LATER AND CANCEL. MAYBE WE CAN FIND OUT HOW THOSE GIRLS OPERATE.

OH, SMART! I'LL MAKE UP A NAME AND SAY I NEED A SITTER FOR MY YOUNGER BROTHER!

COMPETITION, ARE YOU READY? HERE COMES THE BABY-SITTERS CLUB!

RING... RING...

HI, LIZ?

MY NAME IS, UH, CANDY. CANDY KANE.... NO, NO JOKE....

I GOT YOUR FLIER FOR THE BABY-SITTERS AGENCY. I'M SUPPOSED TO SIT FOR MY LITTLE BROTHER TOMORROW, AND... UM...

UH, I JUST GOT ASKED OUT ON A DATE.

!

giggle

FROM 3:00 TO 5:00. HE'S SEVEN YEARS OLD. WILL **YOU** BE SITTING FOR HIM? UH-HUH... OH, I SEE.

hee hee hee

mmmfff!!!

I'LL BE AT 555-2321. OH, BUT ONLY FOR ABOUT TEN MORE MINUTES. THEN I HAVE... I HAVE ANOTHER DATE.... WHO WITH?

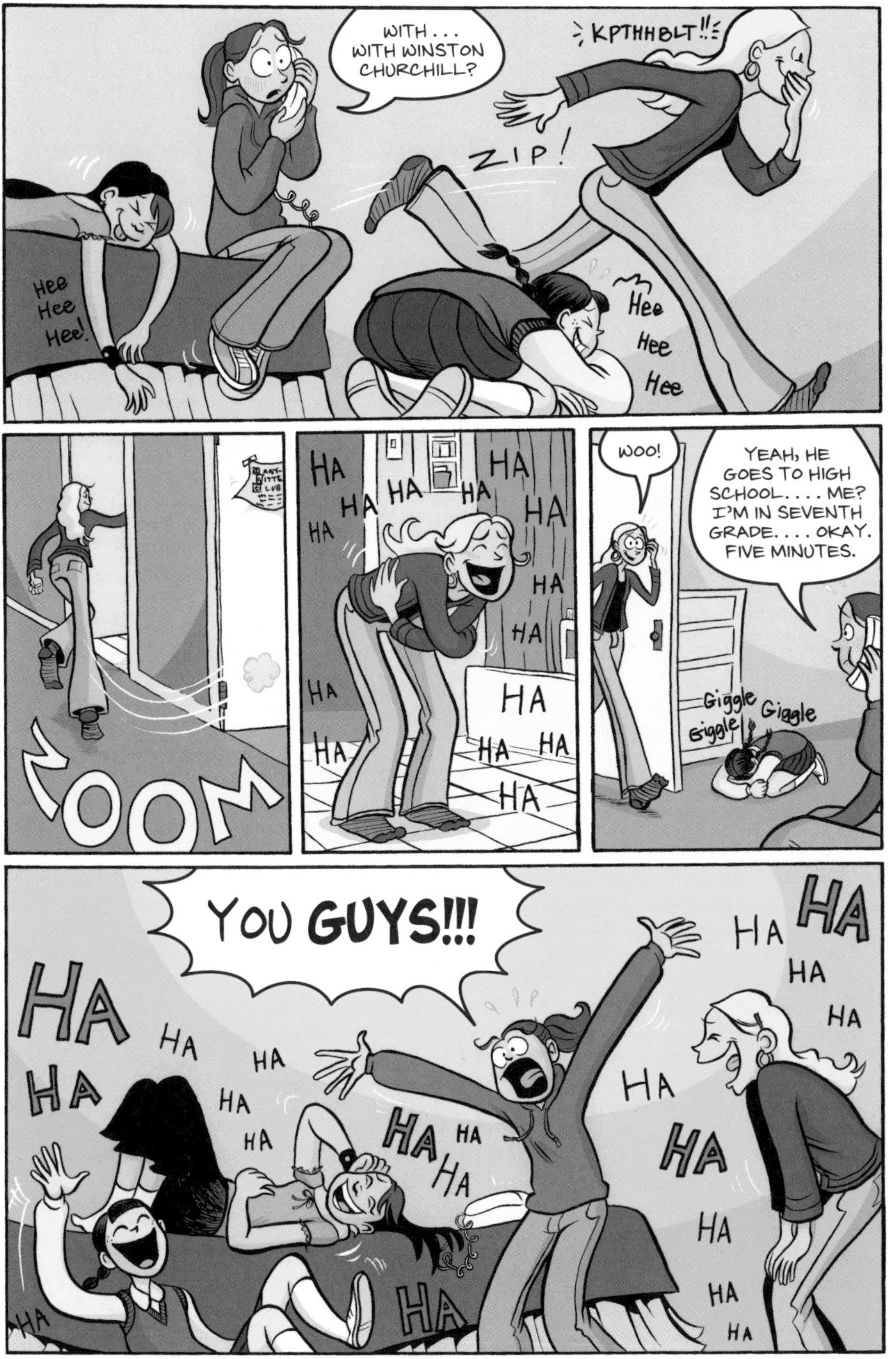
WITH . . . WITH WINSTON CHURCHILL?
KPTHHBLT!!
ZIP!
Hee Hee Hee!
Hee Hee Hee
ZOOM
HA HA HA HA HA HA HA HA HA HA HA HA HA HA HA HA
WOO!
YEAH, HE GOES TO HIGH SCHOOL. . . . ME? I'M IN SEVENTH GRADE. . . . OKAY. FIVE MINUTES.
Giggle Giggle Giggle
YOU GUYS!!!
HA HA HA HA HA HA HA HA HA HA HA HA HA HA HA HA HA HA HA HA HA HA

DON'T **DO** THAT WHEN I'M ON THE **PHONE**!

HA HA HEH...

BUT WINSTON **CHURCHILL**?! THE HIGH SCHOOL GUY YOU'RE **DATING**?!

OKAY, OKAY... I THINK THIS IS HOW THE AGENCY WORKS.

LIZ AND MICHELLE TAKE CALLS FROM CLIENTS, THEN SIMPLY TURN AROUND AND **FIND** THE SITTERS.

NO WONDER THEIR SITTERS ARE SO OLD. ALL LIZ AND MICHELLE HAVE TO DO IS CALL UP OLDER KIDS.

YEAH. WE COULD HAVE THOUGHT OF THAT, I GUESS.

LIZ SEEMED MORE INTERESTED IN MY "DATE" THAN IN FINDING A BABY-SITTER.

RING!

HELLO, THE BABY-SI--... HELLO?

YES, GREAT. **HOW** MANY?... WOW. HOW OLD ARE THEY?... WOW. OKAY.... PATRICIA? SURE, THANKS. I'LL SEE PATRICIA TOMORROW AT THREE.... LATER.

"LATER"?

THAT'S HOW LIZ SAYS GOOD-BYE.

...SO?

SHE ACTUALLY FOUND THREE AVAILABLE SITTERS. I GOT A CHOICE. TWO WERE THIRTEEN YEARS OLD, AND ONE WAS FIFTEEN. ONE WAS EVEN A BOY.

PEOPLE ARE GOING TO LOVE THE AGENCY. I'M NOT KIDDING. WE DON'T OFFER A RANGE OF AGES LIKE THEY DO....

THERE ARE NO BOYS IN OUR CLUB... AND WE CAN'T STAY OUT PAST 10:00, EVEN ON WEEKENDS.

...

STACEY'S DINNER PLATE:

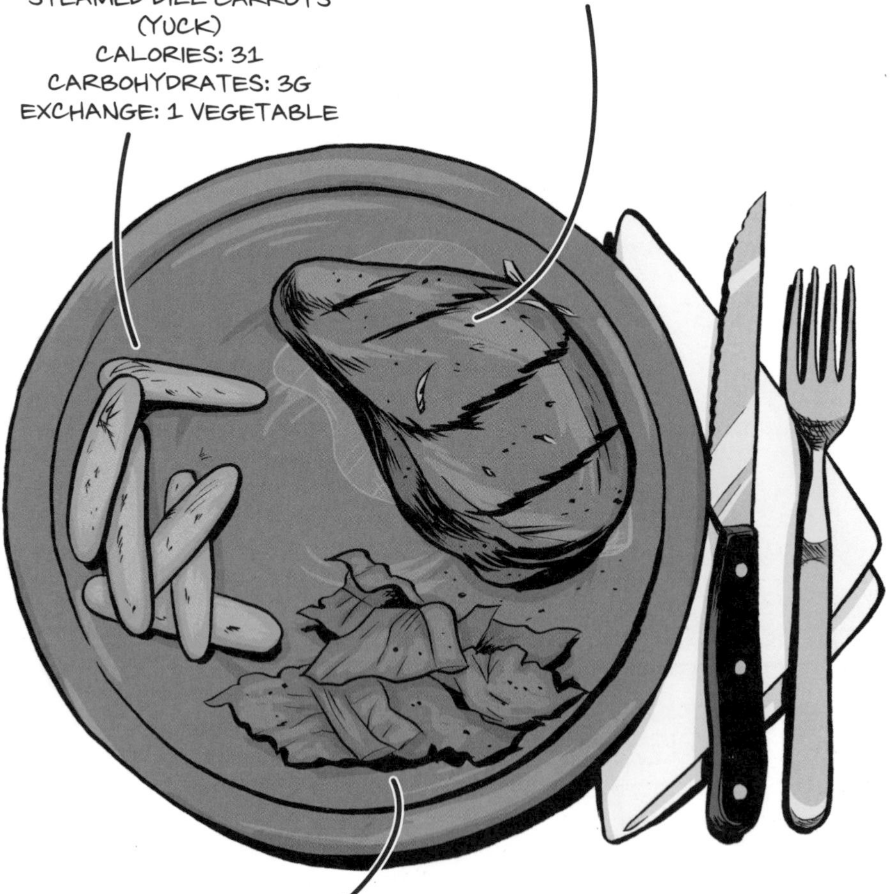
APPLE-GLAZED PORK CHOP
CALORIES: 194
CARBOHYDRATES: 4.8G
EXCHANGE: 1/4 BREAD/STARCH, 1 MEAT
STEAMED DILL CARROTS
(YUCK)
CALORIES: 31
CARBOHYDRATES: 3G
EXCHANGE: 1 VEGETABLE
ROMAINE LETTUCE SALAD
WITH LOW-CAL ITALIAN DRESSING
CALORIES: 39
CARBOHYDRATES: 2.8G
EXCHANGE: 1 VEGETABLE

CHAPTER 3

LATER THAT EVENING...

HONEY, ARE YOU FEELING ALL RIGHT? YOU HAVEN'T EATEN MUCH DINNER.

I'M NOT VERY HUNGRY.

ARE YOUR BLOOD SUGARS RUNNING HIGH?

I WAS 105 BEFORE DINNER, OK?

DO YOU THINK I **WANT** TO MAKE MYSELF GET SICK?

NO...I'M SORRY, HONEY. IT'S JUST THAT...

YOU'VE LOST THREE POUNDS THIS MONTH, AND... ARE YOU **SURE** YOU'RE FEELING ALL RIGHT?

YES. MAYBE I'M MORE ACTIVE NOW THAT I HAVE SOME FRIENDS HERE. MAYBE I NEED TO EAT **MORE.**

BUT YOU JUST SAID YOU WEREN'T HUNGRY. I'LL CALL THE DOCTOR ON MONDAY.

JUST IN CASE.

WHICH ONE?

WELL, I SUPPOSE WE DON'T NEED TO GO ALL THE WAY TO NEW YORK TO SEE DR. WERNER.

WE CAN CALL YOUR DOCTOR IN STONEYBROOK.

GOOD.

BUT, JUST SO YOU KNOW . . .

WE'RE GOING TO SCHEDULE A SERIES OF TESTS WITH A NEW DOCTOR IN NEW YORK AT THE BEGINNING OF DECEMBER.

AW, MOMMM . . .

HONEY, SUPPOSEDLY HE'S WORKING MIRACLES WITH DIABETES.

UNCLE ERIC SAW HIM ON A TV PROGRAM WHERE--

WE'RE GOING TO A DOCTOR BECAUSE UNCLE ERIC SAW HIM ON **TV**?!!

WELL, AND THEN I READ ABOUT HIM IN A MAGAZINE, AND HE SOUNDED VERY IMPRESSIVE.

BUT MOM, WHY?!

WHY DO I HAVE TO SEE ANOTHER DOCTOR?? I'VE BEEN GOING TO DR. WERNER SINCE LAST YEAR. I HAVE DR. FRANK HERE IN STONEYBROOK, AND I LIKE HIM FINE.

THERE'S NO WAY TO TREAT WHAT I'VE GOT, EXCEPT WITH DIET AND INSULIN--

AND THAT'S JUST WHAT WE'RE DOING.

YOUR FATHER AND I WANT THE BEST FOR YOU.

WE'VE **GOT** THE BEST!

IT'S ONLY FOR THREE DAYS.

THREE DAYS?! MOM, I SPENT SIXTH GRADE FALLING FURTHER AND FURTHER BEHIND, WHILE YOU DRAGGED ME FROM DOCTOR TO DOCTOR, LOOKING FOR A MIRACLE! AND YOU'RE GOING TO START DOING IT **AGAIN??**

YOUNG LADY, I DON'T APPRECIATE YOUR TONE OF VOICE.

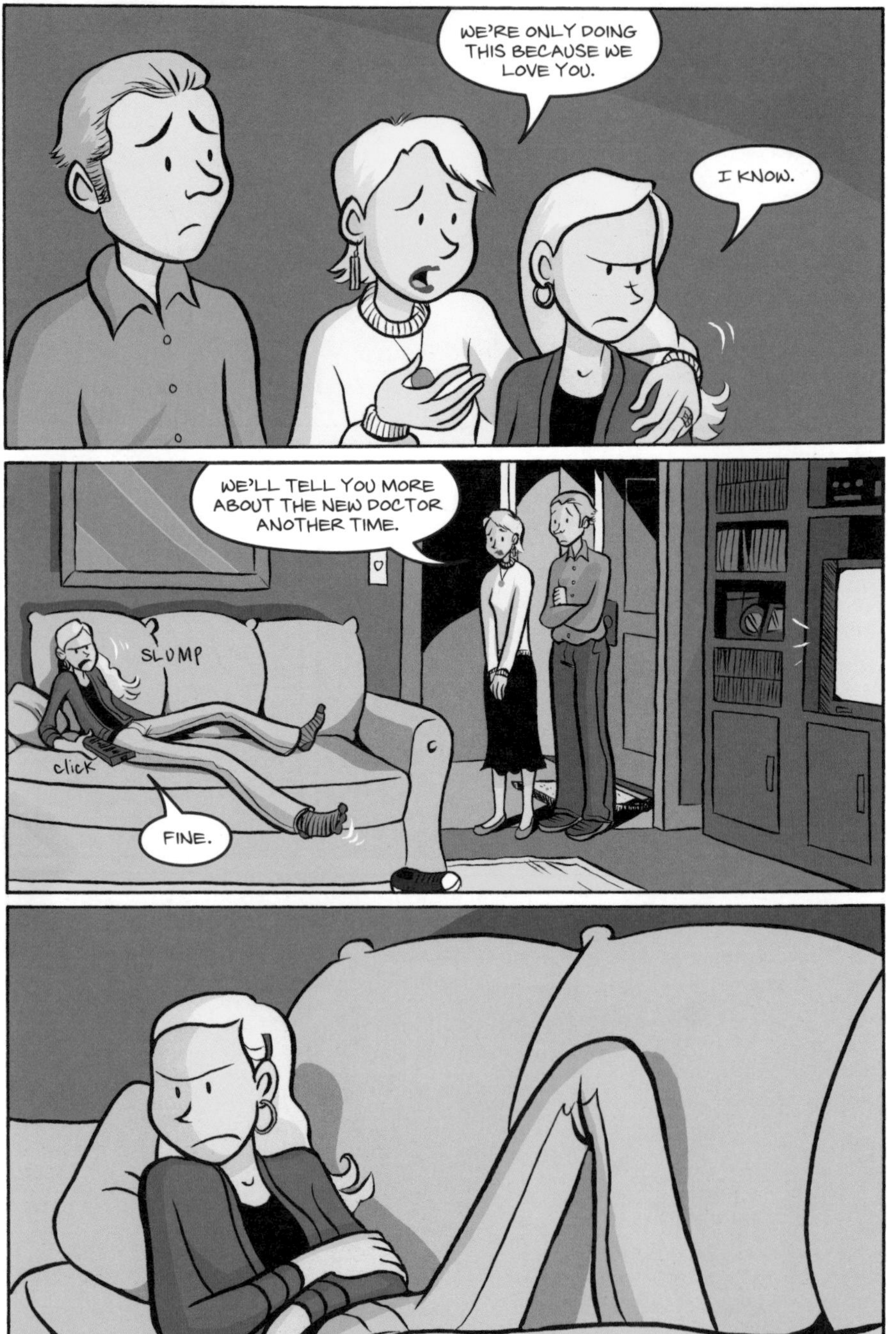
WE'RE ONLY DOING THIS BECAUSE WE LOVE YOU.
I KNOW.
WE'LL TELL YOU MORE ABOUT THE NEW DOCTOR ANOTHER TIME.
SLUMP
click
FINE.

KRISTY CALLED AN EMERGENCY MEETING THE NEXT MORNING. WE GATHERED IN CLAUDIA'S ROOM.

OKAY. I'VE DRAWN UP A LIST OF WAYS TO IMPROVE OURSELVES AS SITTERS AND MAKE US LOOK BETTER TO OUR CLIENTS.

NUMBER ONE . . .

WE'LL DO HOUSEWORK AT NO EXTRA CHARGE.

OH, GROSS.

TWO: WE'LL OFFER SPECIAL DEALS TO OUR BEST CUSTOMERS.

THAT MAKES SENSE.

THREE: WE'LL EACH MAKE UP A KID-KIT TO BRING WITH US WHEN WE SIT.

WHAT'S A KID-KIT?

ANOTHER IDEA I CAME UP WITH. YOU KNOW HOW YOU LIKE GOING TO YOUR FRIENDS' HOUSES BECAUSE YOUR FRIENDS ALWAYS SEEM TO HAVE BETTER **STUFF** THAN YOU DO?

BETTER FOOD, BETTER THINGS TO DO, AND--WHEN YOU WERE LITTLE--BETTER **TOYS?**

OH, YEAH! IN NEW YORK, I HAD THIS FRIEND NAMED LAINE.

I LOVED GOING TO HER APARTMENT, BECAUSE HER MOM WOULD BUY MILKY WAY BARS AND KEEP THEM IN THE FREEZER.

BITING INTO ONE OF THOSE WAS LIKE BITING INTO A FROZEN CHOCOLATE MILKSHA--

UM . . .

WELL, THIS WAS **BEFORE** I GOT SICK. ANYWAY, I KNOW WHAT YOU MEAN.

YEAH!

I LIKED KRISTY'S HOUSE BECAUSE OF HER BIG FAMILY AND THEIR DOG.

AND I LIKED CLAUDIA'S HOUSE BECAUSE HER FAMILY HAD ALL THOSE BOARD GAMES.

WHAT WE REALLY LIKE IS THE CHANGE OF PACE--NEW OR DIFFERENT THINGS. SO EVERY TIME WE SIT, WE'LL BRING THE KIDS SOME OF OUR OWN STUFF--

--JUST TO PLAY WITH WHILE WE'RE SITTING. THE KIDS WILL **WANT** US TO SIT, BECAUSE WE'LL BE LIKE A WALKING TOY STORE!

EACH OF US WILL GET A BOX AND LABEL IT "KID-KIT." WE'LL FILL THEM WITH GAMES, TOYS, AND BOOKS OF OUR OWN.

WE CAN BUY THINGS LIKE PAPER AND CRAYONS, WHICH WE'LL REPLACE FROM TIME TO TIME.

WE CAN USE OUR CLUB DUES FOR THOSE.

RIGHT!

THE KIDS WILL **LOVE** THIS!

OKAY, I HAVE A FEW MORE IDEAS. NUMBER FOUR, LOWER RATES. AND NUMBER FIVE . . .

WE'LL DO WHAT THE AGENCY DOES: TAKE ON LATE JOBS BY GIVING THEM TO OLDER KIDS. MY OLDER BROTHERS BABY-SIT SOMETIMES, AND MAYBE JANINE COULD--

NO!!

KRISTY, THIS IS GETTING OUT OF HAND. THE KID-KIT IS A GOOD IDEA, BUT LOWER RATES? HOUSEWORK? GIVING AWAY OUR JOBS?

NO, NO, NO. IF THAT'S WHAT THIS CLUB IS GOING TO BECOME, THEN I DON'T WANT TO BE IN IT.

ME NEITHER.

YOU GUYS, I DON'T WANT THE CLUB TO FALL APART. WE **CAN'T** LET LIZ AND MICHELLE BEAT US.

I THINK WE SHOULD USE TWO OF KRISTY'S IDEAS: THE KID-KITS AND THE SPECIAL DEALS.

BUT WE SHOULD SAVE THE OTHER IDEAS AS LAST RESORTS.

THAT'S FOR SURE.

WELL, WE CAN AT LEAST START MAKING THE KID-KITS. CLAUD, DO YOU HAVE ANY EMPTY BOXES?

OH, YEAH! LET ME GO GRAB SOME FROM THE BASEMENT.

WAIT RIGHT HERE.

I HAVE GLITTER, AND FABRIC, AND PAINTS, AND ALL SORTS OF THINGS WE CAN DECORATE THEM WITH!

COOL!

TUG

ART SUPPII

THESE WILL BE THE BEST BOXES EVER!!

KID K

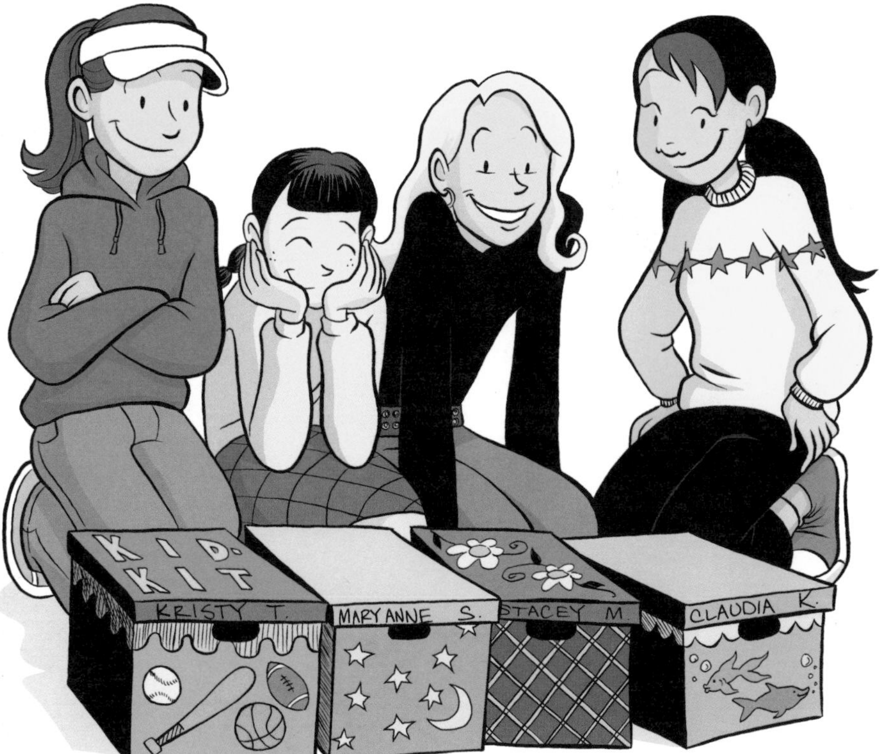
KID-KIT
KRISTY T.
MARY ANNE S.
STACEY M.
CLAUDIA K.

November 10

Monday I had a sitting job for Charlotte Johanssen. I love sitting for Charlotte, she's one of my very favorite kids. And her mother, Dr. Johanssen, is a Doctor at Stoneybrook Medical Center, so I like talking to her — she always asks me how I'm doing and how I feel about my treatments. Today was no different, except for what happened near the end of the afternoon . . .

Stacey

CHAPTER 4

MONDAY AFTERNOON...

KNOCK

STACEY

HELLO, STACEY.

HI, DR. JOHANSSEN.

HOW HAVE YOU BEEN FEELING?

HUNGRY. AND I'VE LOST SOME WEIGHT.

ANY PROBLEMS WITH YOUR INSULIN OR YOUR BLOOD SUGAR LEVELS?

NOPE. I THINK I JUST NEED TO EAT MORE.

AFTER ALL, I **AM** TWELVE.

THAT SOUNDS SENSIBLE.

STACEY! HI, STACEY!

HI, CHARLOTTE!

WHAT'S IN THE BOX?

SOMETHING SPECIAL. I'LL OPEN IT AS SOON AS YOUR MOM LEAVES.

MOM, GO, GO!

IS THAT A HINT?

NOW??

"KID-KIT." IT'S PRETTY. CAN I OPEN IT?

GO AHEAD!

OH, NEAT . . . CRAYONS, CHALK, PLAY-DOH . . . CHUTES AND LADDERS . . .

THE CRICKET IN TIMES SQUARE. CAN WE READ THIS BOOK?

SURE!

WE CAN READ A LITTLE BIT EACH TIME I BABY-SIT. AND I CAN TELL YOU ABOUT WHEN I LIVED IN THE CITY, SINCE THAT'S WHERE THE BOOK TAKES PLACE.

GOODY!

HEY, I KNOW YOU WANT TO PLAY WITH THE KID-KIT, BUT I ALSO HAVE ANOTHER IDEA.

WHAT?

WE COULD WALK DOWNTOWN. IT'S PRETTY WARM OUT FOR A NOVEMBER AFTERNOON!

WE COULD LOOK IN THE STORE WINDOWS, FIND OUT WHAT'S PLAYING AT THE THEATER... MAYBE STOP AT THE PLAYGROUND ON THE WAY HOME?

...

...DOWNTOWN. BUT ONLY IF YOU PROMISE TO BRING THE KID-KIT BACK.

PROMISE.

OOH, ACORNS!

I SHOULD SAVE THESE. THEN IF I GOT A PET SQUIRREL, I COULD FEED HIM.

WHAT WOULD YOU DO WITH A PET SQUIRREL?

TALK TO HIM.

DON'T YOU HAVE FRIENDS YOU CAN TALK TO, CHARLOTTE?

I MEAN, **PEOPLE** FRIENDS?

NO.

THE KIDS IN MY CLASS DON'T LIKE ME. AND I DON'T LIKE THEM.

WHY DON'T YOU LIKE THEM?

BECAUSE THEY DON'T LIKE **ME**.

HMM.

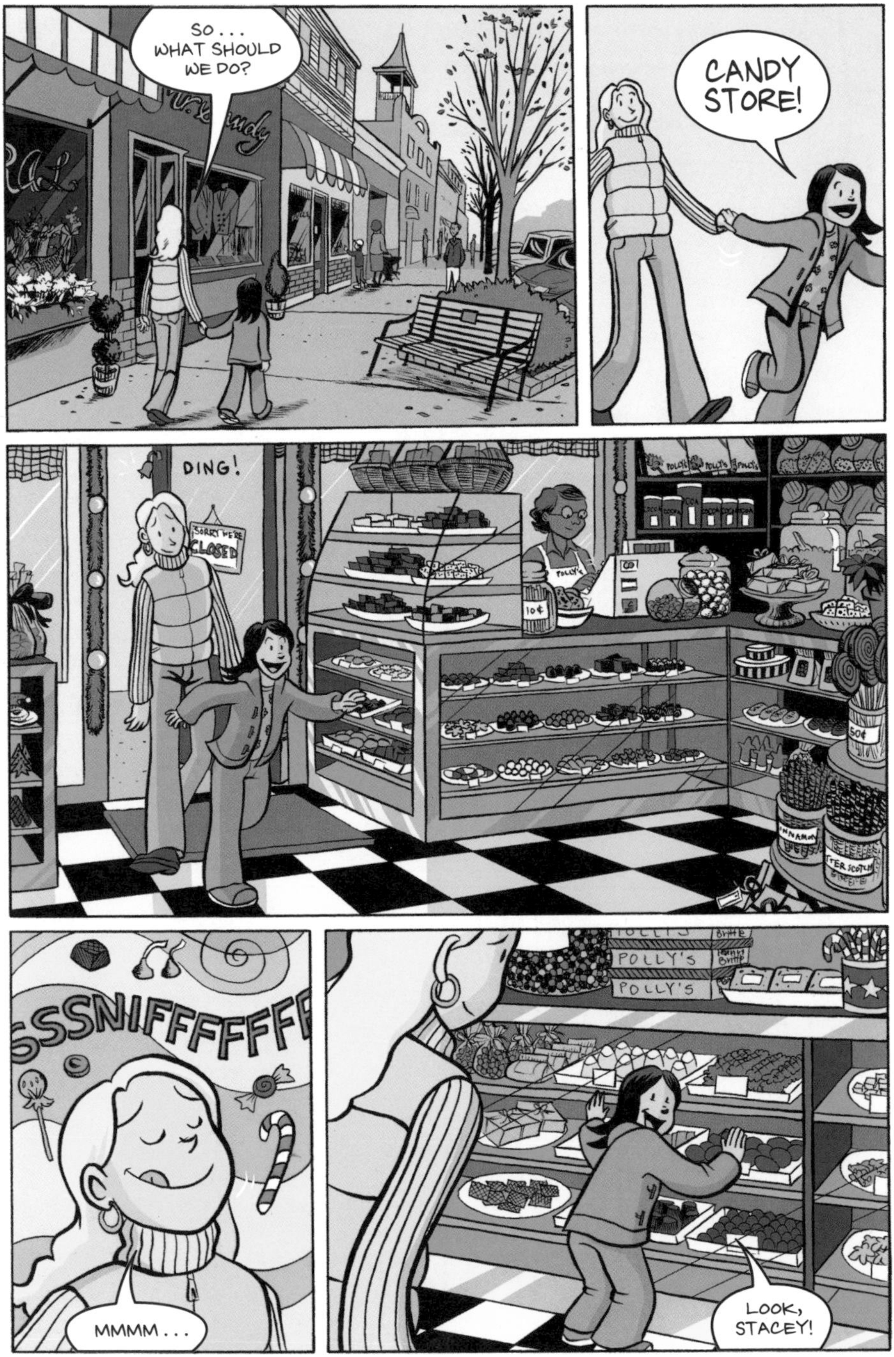
SO . . .
WHAT SHOULD
WE DO?
CANDY
STORE!
DING!
SORRY WE'RE
CLOSED
10¢
50¢
POLLY'S
SSSNIFFFFFF
MMMM . . .
POLLY'S
POLLY'S
LOOK,
STACEY!

COULD WE GET JUST ONE THING? ONE THING EACH, PLEASE?

GASP!

I COULDN'T BELIEVE WHAT I'D ALMOST DONE.

...BETTER NOT.

Fumble

IT'S TOO CLOSE TO DINNER. YOUR MOM DOESN'T LIKE YOU EATING SWEETS, ANYWAY.

I KNOW, I JUST THOUGHT...

10¢

I WANTED A TREAT, TOO. YOU'RE NOT THE ONLY ONE WHO'S NOT SUPPOSED TO EAT SWEETS.

DING

BUT WE STILL HAVE ENOUGH TIME TO GO TO THE PLAYGROUND BEFORE WE HEAD HOME.

OKAY!

...NO.

IT'S NOT DARK YET. THERE'S OTHER KIDS THERE.

NO. I WANT TO GO HOME.

HEY, THERE'S **CHAR**-CHAR!

TEACHER'S PET! SMARTY-PANTS!

CHAR-CHAR! TEACHER'S PET!

I AM NOT THE TEACHER'S PET!!

HA HA!

CHARLOTTE!

GO AWAY.

I CAN'T GO AWAY. I'M YOUR BABY-SITTER.

HOW COME THOSE KIDS TEASED YOU?

TROT

I DON'T WANT TO TALK ABOUT IT.

HEY, LISTEN. I GOT TEASED A **LOT** LAST YEAR.

IN NEW YORK?

YUP.

WHO TEASED **YOU?**

MY BEST FRIEND. WELL, SHE **USED** TO BE MY BEST FRIEND.

WHY DID SHE TEASE YOU?

IT'S A LONG STORY.

YOU DON'T WANT TO TALK ABOUT IT EITHER?

I GUESS NOT.

LOOK AT **THAT!!**

HI!!

I'M LIZ LEWIS, PRESIDENT OF THE BABY-SITTERS AGENCY.

I HOPE YOU'LL CALL ME IF YOU EVER NEED A SITTER FOR YOUR LITTLE SISTER.

THE NUMBER'S ON THE BALLOON. LATER!

"THE BABY-SITTERS AGENCY. CALL LIZ LEWIS OR MICHELLE PATTERSON: 555-7548."

MORE BABY-SITTERS? WHAT'S AN AGENCY, STACEY?

IT'S ANOTHER LONG STORY.

COME ON. LET'S GO HOME.

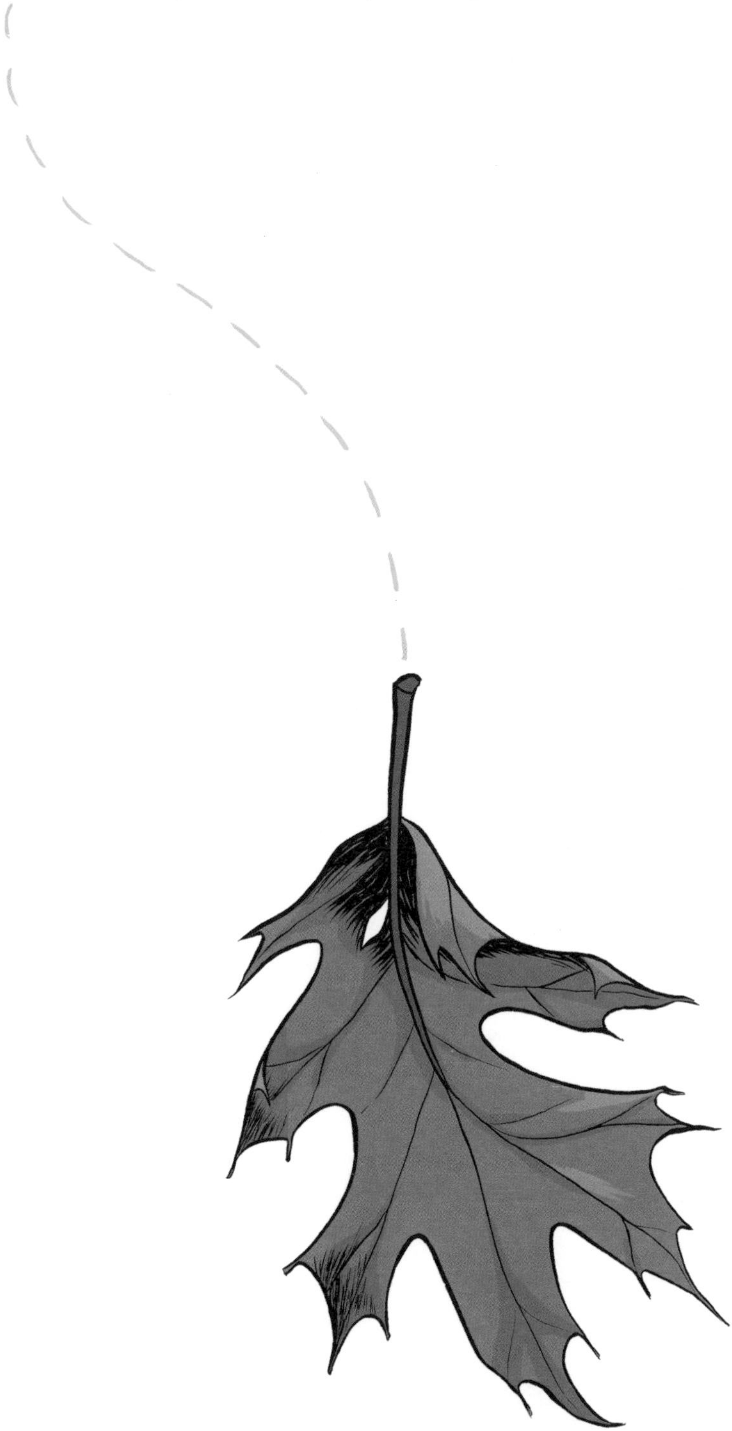

Sunday, November 23

It is just one week since Liz Lewis and Michelle Patterson sent around their fliers. Usually, our club gets about fourteen or fifteen jobs a week. Since last Monday, we've had SEVEN. That's why I'm writing in our notebook. This book is supposed to be a diary of our baby-sitting jobs, so each of us can write up our problems and experiences for the other club members to read. But the Baby-sitters Agency is the biggest problem we've ever had, and I plan to keep track of it in our notebook.

We better do something fast.

— Kristy

CHAPTER 5

AFTER SCHOOL THE NEXT DAY, THE FOUR OF US WALKED HOME TOGETHER.

BALLOONS! WHY DIDN'T **WE** THINK OF BALLOONS?!

YEAH, IT'S TOO BAD.

I KNOW.

YOU GUYS WANT TO COME OVER FOR A WHILE?

GOTTA WORK ON MY OIL PAINTING.

AND I HAVE TO BAKE CRANBERRY BREAD FOR THANKSGIVING DINNER.

I'LL COME OVER, KRISTY.

YEAH, **YOU** JUST WANNA SEE MY BROTHER SAM. . . .

HUH, THE DOOR'S OPEN. . . . WEIRD.

I HOPE MY LITTLE BROTHER DIDN'T GET HOME FIRST. . . . **DAVID MICHAEL??**

MOM!! WHAT ARE **YOU** DOING HOME?!

COME SEE WHO ELSE IS HERE!

WHO?

JAMIE! HI!

HI-HI!

MY MOMMY'S HAVING A BABY!

HAVING THE BABY? **NOW?!**

KRISTY, I KNOW YOU GIRLS HAD PLANS FOR HELPING THE NEWTONS OUT, BUT THE BABY STARTED TO COME LATE THIS MORNING.

MR. NEWTON PHONED ME AT WORK, AND THEY DROPPED JAMIE OFF AT MY OFFICE ON THE WAY TO THE HOSPITAL.

AND NOW I'M LEAVING JAMIE IN YOUR CAPABLE HANDS AND GOING BACK TO THE OFFICE FOR A FEW HOURS.

BUT, MOM, WAIT!

WHAT DID MRS. NEWTON HAVE??

SORRY, NO WORD YET. MR. NEWTON PROMISED TO CALL AS SOON AS THE BABY'S BORN.

BUTTON BUTTON

WELL, HOW LONG DOES IT TAKE TO HAVE A BABY?

IT DEPENDS ON THE BABY. YOU TOOK 24 HOURS.

WHAT?!

HERE'S THE KEY TO THE NEWTONS' HOUSE. I'LL PAY YOU FOR SITTING THIS AFTERNOON.... I'LL BE HOME BY 6:30.

SO, JAMIE, WHAT DO YOU THINK? YOU'RE GOING TO BE A BIG BROTHER PRETTY SOON.

WHAT DO YOU WANT? A BROTHER OR A SISTER?

BROTHER.

YOU **KNOW** . . .

BEING A BIG BROTHER IS PRETTY IMPORTANT.

?

I THINK YOU OUGHT TO HAVE A BIG-BROTHER PARTY!

A PARTY? FOR **ME**?!

YEAH! WE SHOULD CELEBRATE OUR FAVORITE BIG BROTHER . . . **YOU!!**

WE'LL INVITE EVERYONE!

WE CAN PLAY MUSICAL RUG!

AND HAVE AN EGG RACE!

Beep Beep

CLAUDIA'S ON HER WAY OVER, MARY ANNE WILL BE HERE AS SOON AS SHE FINISHES THE BATTER FOR HER CRANBERRY BREAD, AND MALLORY PIKE IS BRINGING HER LITTLE SISTERS, CLAIRE AND MARGO.

CHOP CHOP

OH BOY!

GO PUT A CD ON IN THE REC ROOM, GET OUT SOME PAPER . . .

TWENTY MINUTES LATER . . .

RINGGG!

KRISTY! PHONE!

IT'S MR. NEWTON.

JAMIE, IT'S YOUR DADDY! COME ON!

HELLO. DADDY? . . . FINE. WE'RE HAVING A PARTY. . . . OH. OKAY. 'BYE.

MR. NEWTON? WHAT IS IT? WHAT IS--

IT'S A GIRL.

GASP!!

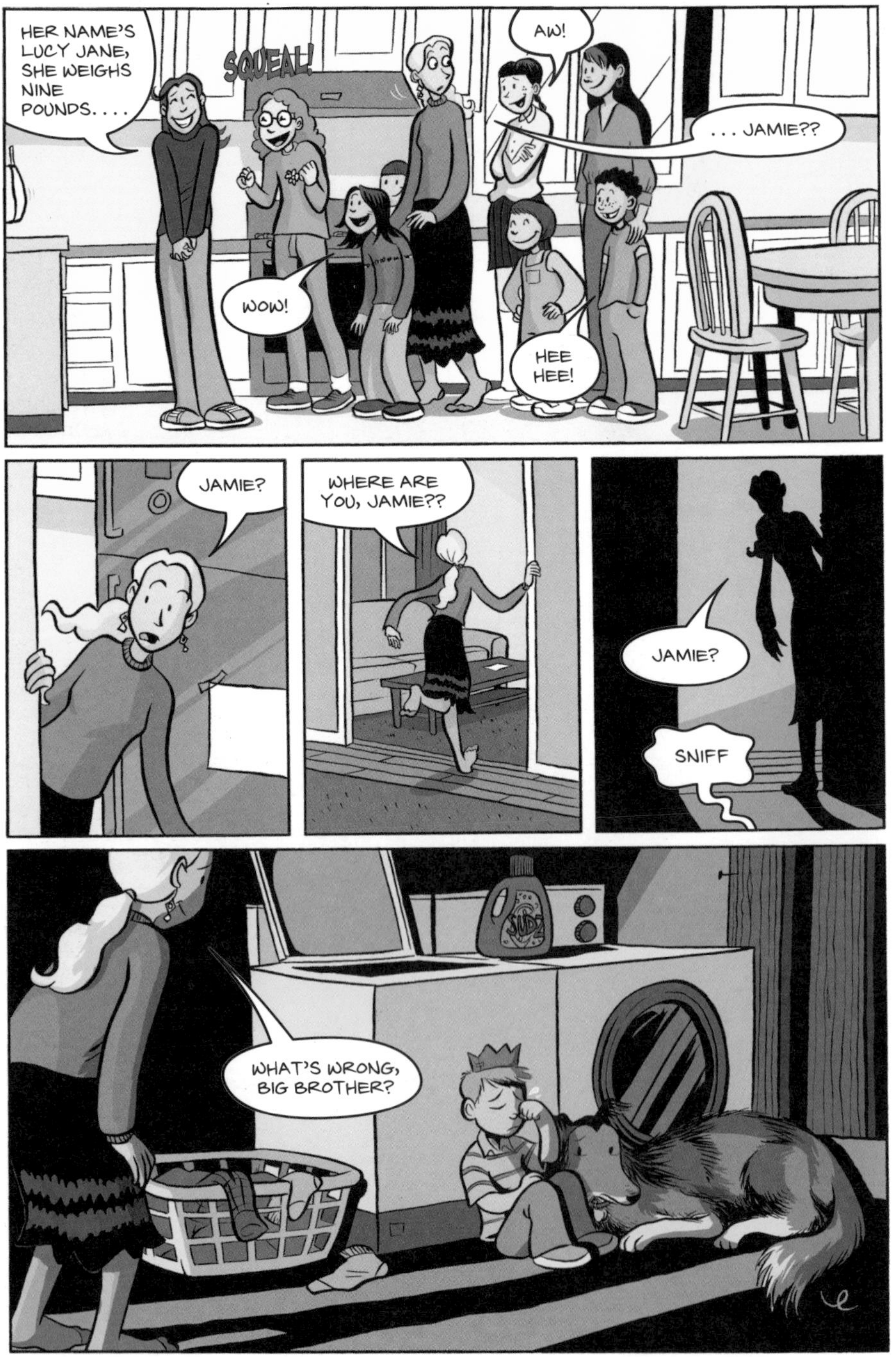
HER NAME'S LUCY JANE, SHE WEIGHS NINE POUNDS. . . .
SQUEAL!
AW!
. . . JAMIE??
WOW!
HEE HEE!
JAMIE?
WHERE ARE YOU, JAMIE??
JAMIE?
SNIFF
WHAT'S WRONG, BIG BROTHER?

THE BABY'S HERE.

AND YOU WANTED A BOY INSTEAD OF A GIRL, RIGHT?

I DUNNO.

EVERY-THING'S CHANGING, HUH?

UH-HUH . . .

KRISTY CAN'T BABY-SIT ME ANYMORE.

WAIT A MINUTE, JAMIE . . . WHAT DO YOU MEAN??

MOMMY CALLED A GIRL AND SAID, "WE NEED AN OLDER SITTER FOR THE NEW BABY."

WAS THE GIRL NAMED LIZ LEWIS?

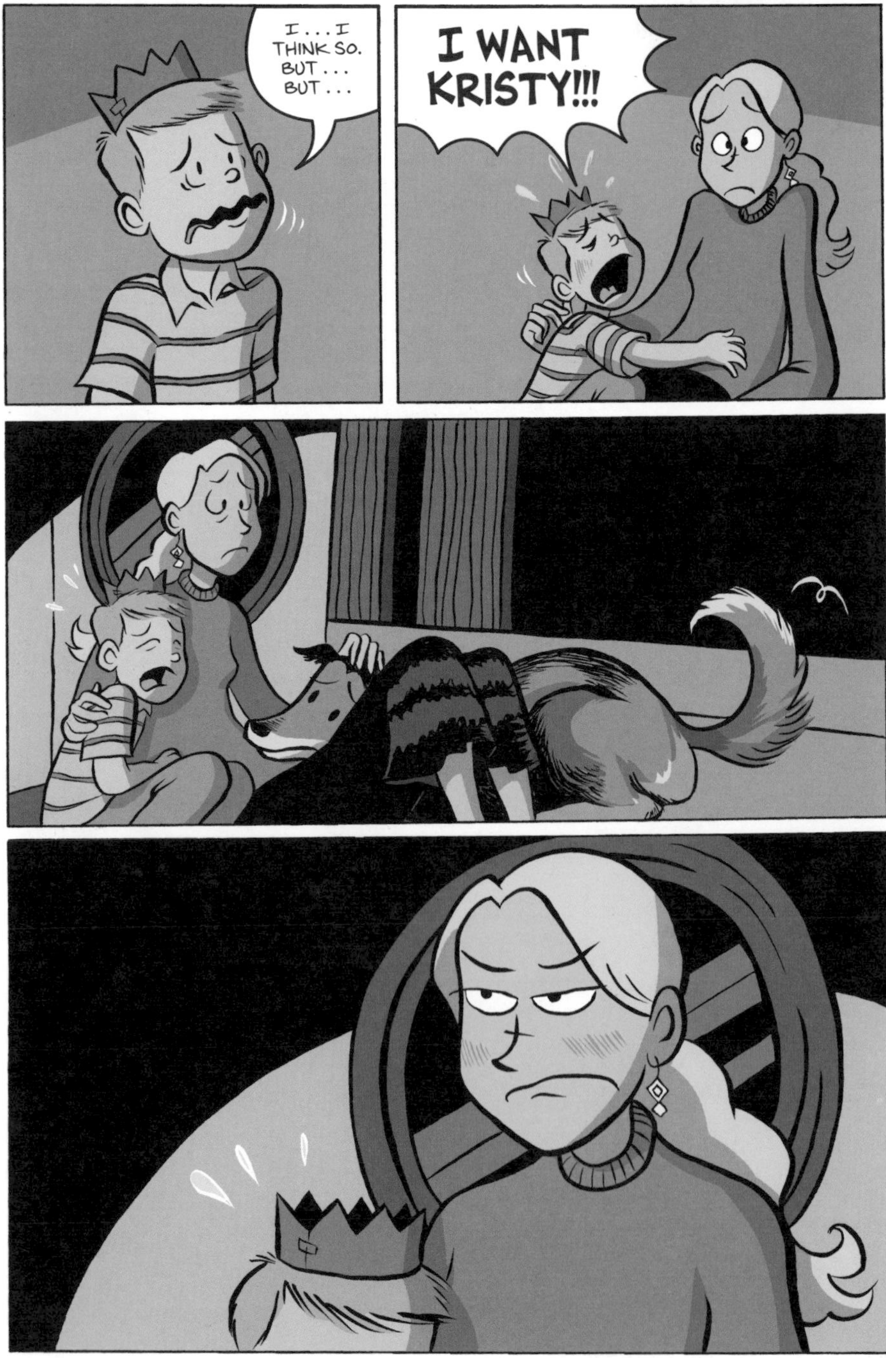
I . . . I
THINK SO.
BUT . . .
BUT . . .
I WANT
KRISTY!!!

CHAPTER 6

TUESDAY MORNING...

...BUT ISN'T IT POSSIBLE JAMIE WAS MISTAKEN? HE'S ONLY THREE. WE DON'T KNOW FOR SURE THAT IT WAS LIZ LEWIS.

YEAH!

I GUESS IT MAKES SENSE THE NEWTONS WOULD WANT SOMEONE OLDER THAN 12 TO WATCH A NEW BABY...

BUT... BUT...

WHAT'S THIS?

LOOK AT THIS. "WANT TO EARN FAST MONEY THE EASY WAY? JOIN THE BABY-SITTERS AGENCY. WE DO THE HARDEST PART--LET THE AGENCY FIND JOBS **FOR** YOU!!"

51

CRUMPLE

CRUNCH

BATHROOM. **NOW.**

I'M SORRY, KRISTY.... I GUESS YOU WERE RIGHT.

WE **DO** NEED TO TAKE SOME EXTREME MEASURES.

WHAT SHOULD WE DO ABOUT THE AGENCY?

TRASH

I THINK OUR BEST BET IS TO FIND SOME NEW MEMBERS FOR THE CLUB.

WE CAN START BY ASKING SOME EIGHTH GRADERS HERE AT OUR SCHOOL.

DO WE **HAVE** TO?

AWW...

WE'VE ONLY HAD THREE JOBS BETWEEN THE FOUR OF US ALL WEEK!

I HAVEN'T EVEN SPOKEN TO DR. OR MR. JOHANSSEN SINCE THE LAST TIME I SAT FOR CHARLOTTE.

YOU SEE?

SO, WE INCREASE OUR RANKS. AGREED?

RINNNNNNG!

GIRLS

AGREED.

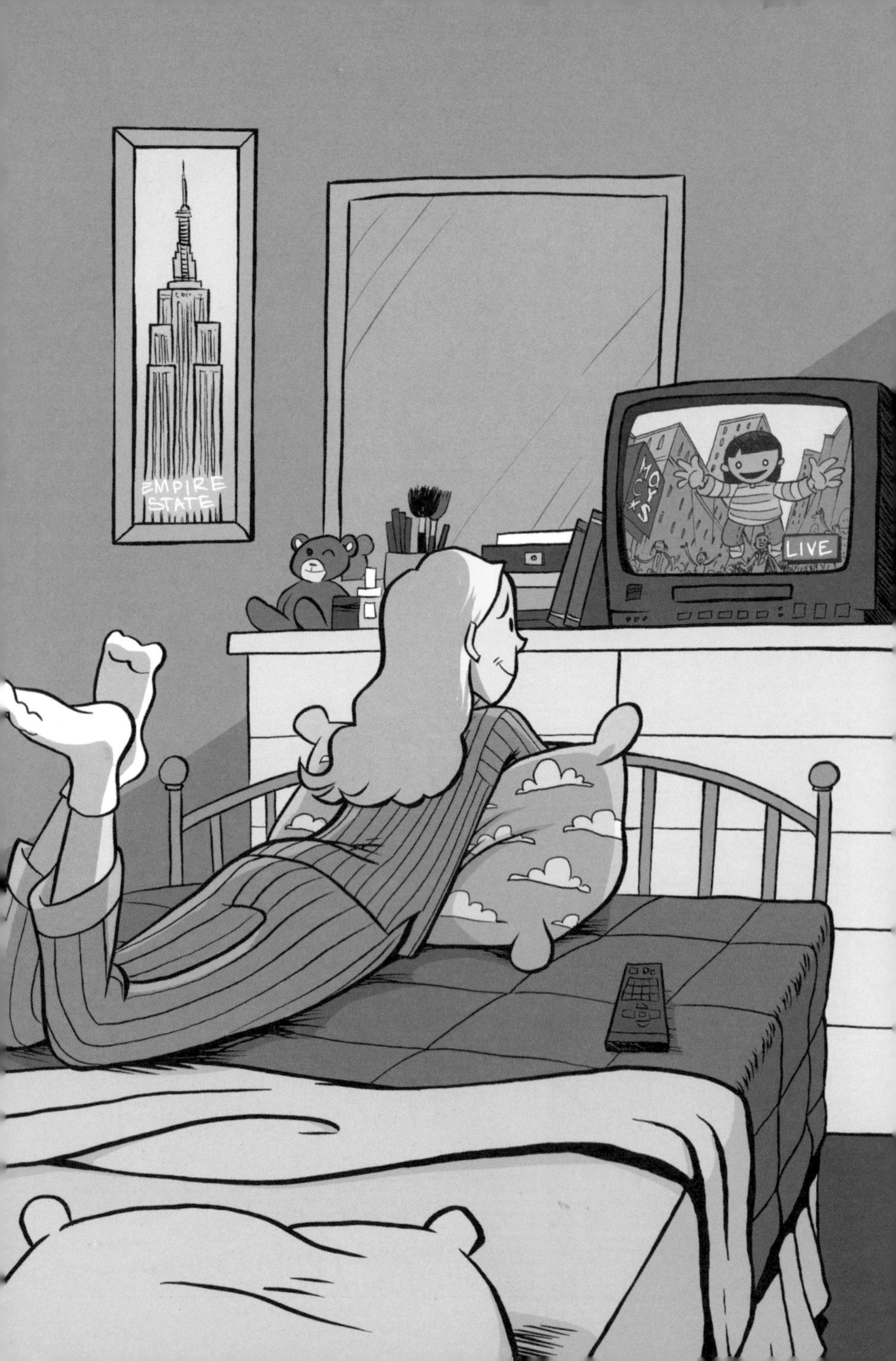
EMPIRE STATE
LIVE

THANKSGIVING WAS ACTUALLY KIND OF FUN.

IT EVEN SNOWED A LITTLE.

IT WAS THE DAY **AFTER** THANKSGIVING THAT MY PARENTS DECIDED TO HIT ME WITH THE NEWS:

SHOULD WE TELL HER NOW, HONEY?

TELL ME **WHAT?!**

WE AREN'T **MOVING** AGAIN, ARE WE?!

HEAVENS, NO.

WE'VE SCHEDULED YOUR TESTS WITH THE NEW DOCTOR, BUT THEY'LL BE A LITTLE LATER IN THE MONTH THAN WE THOUGHT....

NEAR CHRISTMAS?!

WE'LL LEAVE FOR NEW YORK ON FRIDAY, THE TWELFTH, AND PROBABLY RETURN ON WEDNESDAY, THE SEVENTEENTH.

THAT'S **FIVE** DAYS!! YOU SAID WE'D ONLY BE GONE FOR THREE!!

YOU'LL ONLY MISS THREE DAYS OF SCHOOL.... YOU **WILL** SPEND A LOT OF TIME AT THE DOCTOR'S CLINIC, BUT WE'LL HAVE EVENINGS AND ALL OF SUNDAY FREE.

HMPH.

WE CAN GO CHRISTMAS SHOPPING, SEE THE TREE AT ROCKEFELLER CENTER...

AND...

...I GOT TICKETS TO THE SUNDAY PERFORMANCE OF "PARIS MAGIC."

PARIS MAGIC!! REALLY?! WOW! I'VE WANTED TO SEE THAT FOR AGES.... THANKS, DAD.

THINK OF IT, STACEY. CHRISTMASTIME IN NEW YORK. YOU ALWAYS LIKED THE CITY BEST AT THAT SEASON.

I GUESS.... SO WHAT DOES DR. WERNER THINK OF... WHAT'S THE NAME OF THE NEW DOCTOR?

DR. BARNES.

WHAT DOES DR. WERNER THINK OF THIS DR. BARNES?

...SHE DOESN'T KNOW ABOUT DR. BARNES YET.

MO-OM! CAN'T WE CHECK WITH DR. WERNER FIRST? WHAT'S SO SPECIAL ABOUT DR. BARNES? WHY DO I HAVE TO SEE HIM? THIS IS SO UNFAIR!

STACEY, YOU'RE NOT IN CHARGE HERE. YOUR MOTHER AND I MAKE THE DECISIONS.

DECISIONS ABOUT **ME. MY** BODY.

I DON'T FEEL GOOD.

MAYBE YOUR SUGAR'S LOW? WHEN WAS YOUR LAST INJECTION?

I'LL GET YOU AN APPLE. DO YOU WANT SOME PEANUT BUTTER WITH IT? STACEY, **TELL** ME IF YOU NEED A SNACK....

WHAT I **NEED** IS FOR YOU TO JUST LEAVE ME ALONE!!

I BABY-SAT FOR CHARLOTTE ON SATURDAY AFTERNOON, MY FIRST JOB IN OVER A WEEK!

AND WHEN HER MOTHER GOT HOME, WE HAD A CHANCE TO TALK.

DR. JOHANSSEN? MOM AND DAD WANT TO TAKE ME TO **ANOTHER** NEW DOCTOR IN NEW YORK!

IT'S A CLINIC MY UNCLE HEARD ABOUT ON TV.

TV?? DO YOU KNOW THE DOCTOR'S NAME?

UM, DR. BARNES.

OH, NO.

WHAT? DO YOU KNOW HIM?

NOT PERSONALLY, BUT I'VE HEARD OF HIM. HE'S A FAD DOCTOR WHO JUST HAPPENS TO BE GETTING A LOT OF PUBLICITY RIGHT NOW.

I KNEW IT, I KNEW IT.

NOW, DON'T WORRY...

DR. BARNES ISN'T GOING TO HARM YOU, FROM WHAT I'VE HEARD. HE WON'T TOUCH YOUR INSULIN LEVELS.

BUT WHAT HE PROBABLY **WILL** DO...

...IS RECOMMEND ALL SORTS OF EXPENSIVE PROGRAMS AND THERAPIES.

THERAPIES? LIKE WHAT?

OH, EVERYTHING. SENDING YOU TO A PSYCHIATRIST... EXERCISE PROGRAMS... RECREATIONAL THERAPY...

HE MAY EVEN RECOMMEND THAT YOU CHANGE SCHOOLS, SO YOU CAN GET INDIVIDUALIZED INSTRUCTION.

ERK!

CHANGE SCHOOLS?! NO!!

THERE'S NOTHING REALLY **WRONG** WITH ANY OF THOSE THINGS, BUT IT'S MY BELIEF THAT NO SPECIAL PROGRAM IS GOING TO RID YOUR BODY OF DIABETES.

DR. JOHANSSEN, YOU HAVE TO HELP ME!

STACEY, I'D LIKE TO, BUT I BARELY KNOW YOUR PARENTS.

BUT YOU KNOW **ME,** AND YOU'RE A DOCTOR.

YES, BUT I'M NOT **YOUR** DOCTOR.

PLEASE?

LET ME THINK. I CAN'T INTERVENE DIRECTLY, BUT. . . I PROMISE I WON'T LET YOU LEAVE FOR NEW YORK WITHOUT DOING **SOMETHING.**

OKAY?

IT WAS HARD TO BELIEVE I'D BE IN NEW YORK AGAIN SO SOON.

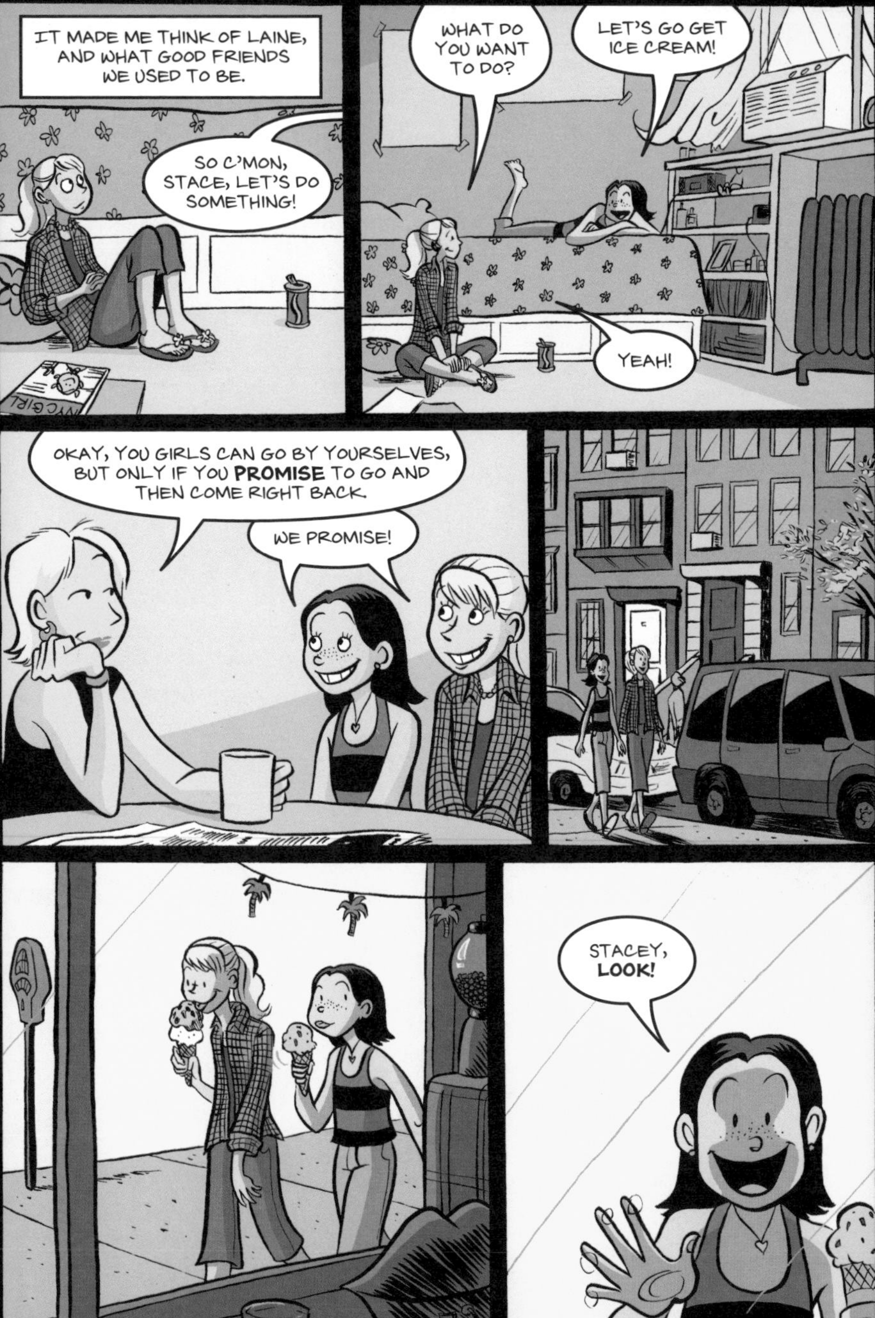
IT MADE ME THINK OF LAINE, AND WHAT GOOD FRIENDS WE USED TO BE.
SO C'MON, STACE, LET'S DO SOMETHING!
NYC GIRL
WHAT DO YOU WANT TO DO?
LET'S GO GET ICE CREAM!
YEAH!
OKAY, YOU GIRLS CAN GO BY YOURSELVES, BUT ONLY IF YOU **PROMISE** TO GO AND THEN COME RIGHT BACK.
WE PROMISE!
STACEY, **LOOK!**

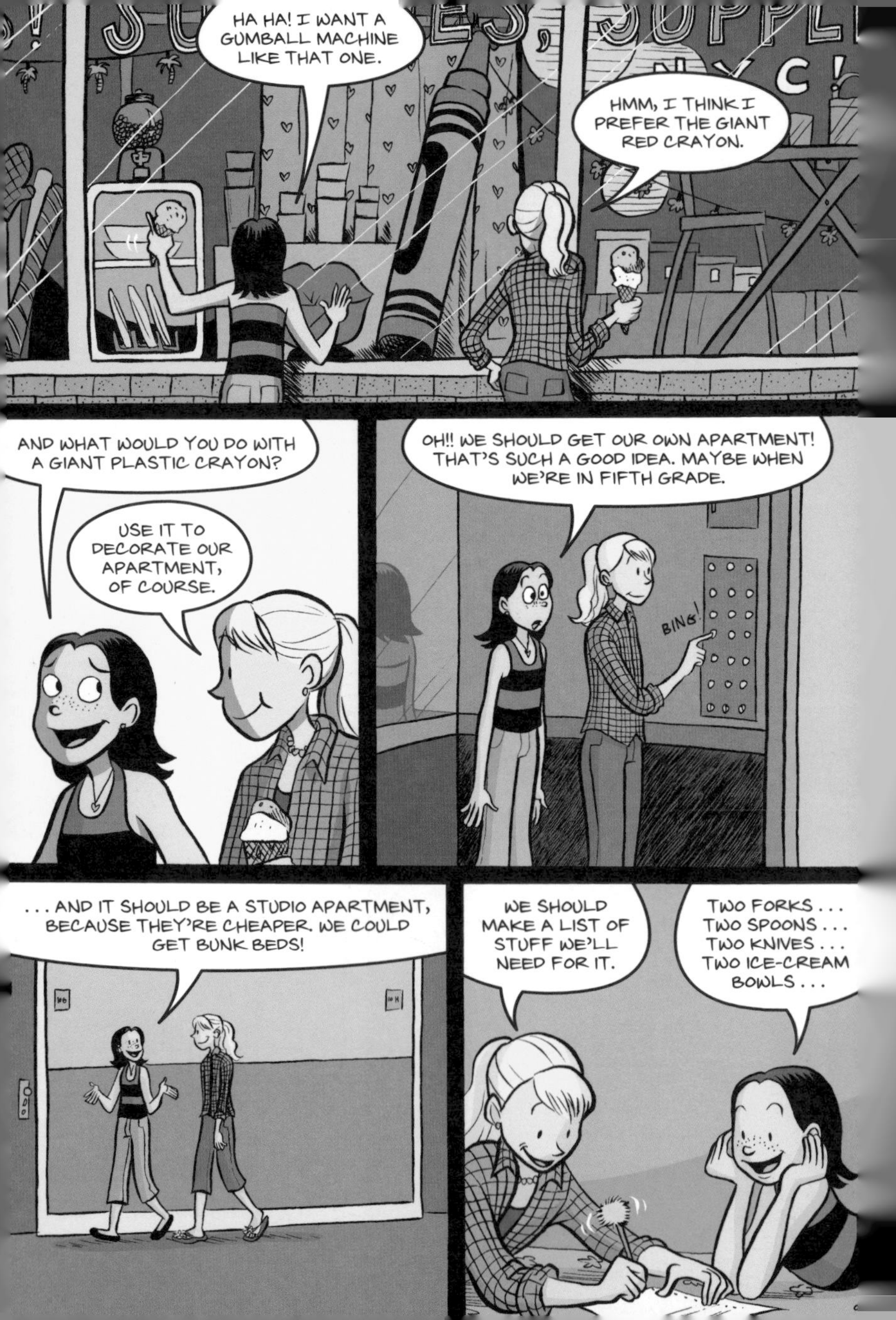
HA HA! I WANT A GUMBALL MACHINE LIKE THAT ONE.
HMM, I THINK I PREFER THE GIANT RED CRAYON.
AND WHAT WOULD YOU DO WITH A GIANT PLASTIC CRAYON?
USE IT TO DECORATE OUR APARTMENT, OF COURSE.
OH!! WE SHOULD GET OUR OWN APARTMENT! THAT'S SUCH A GOOD IDEA. MAYBE WHEN WE'RE IN FIFTH GRADE.
BING!
. . . AND IT SHOULD BE A STUDIO APARTMENT, BECAUSE THEY'RE CHEAPER. WE COULD GET BUNK BEDS!
WE SHOULD MAKE A LIST OF STUFF WE'LL NEED FOR IT.
TWO FORKS . . . TWO SPOONS . . . TWO KNIVES . . . TWO ICE-CREAM BOWLS . . .

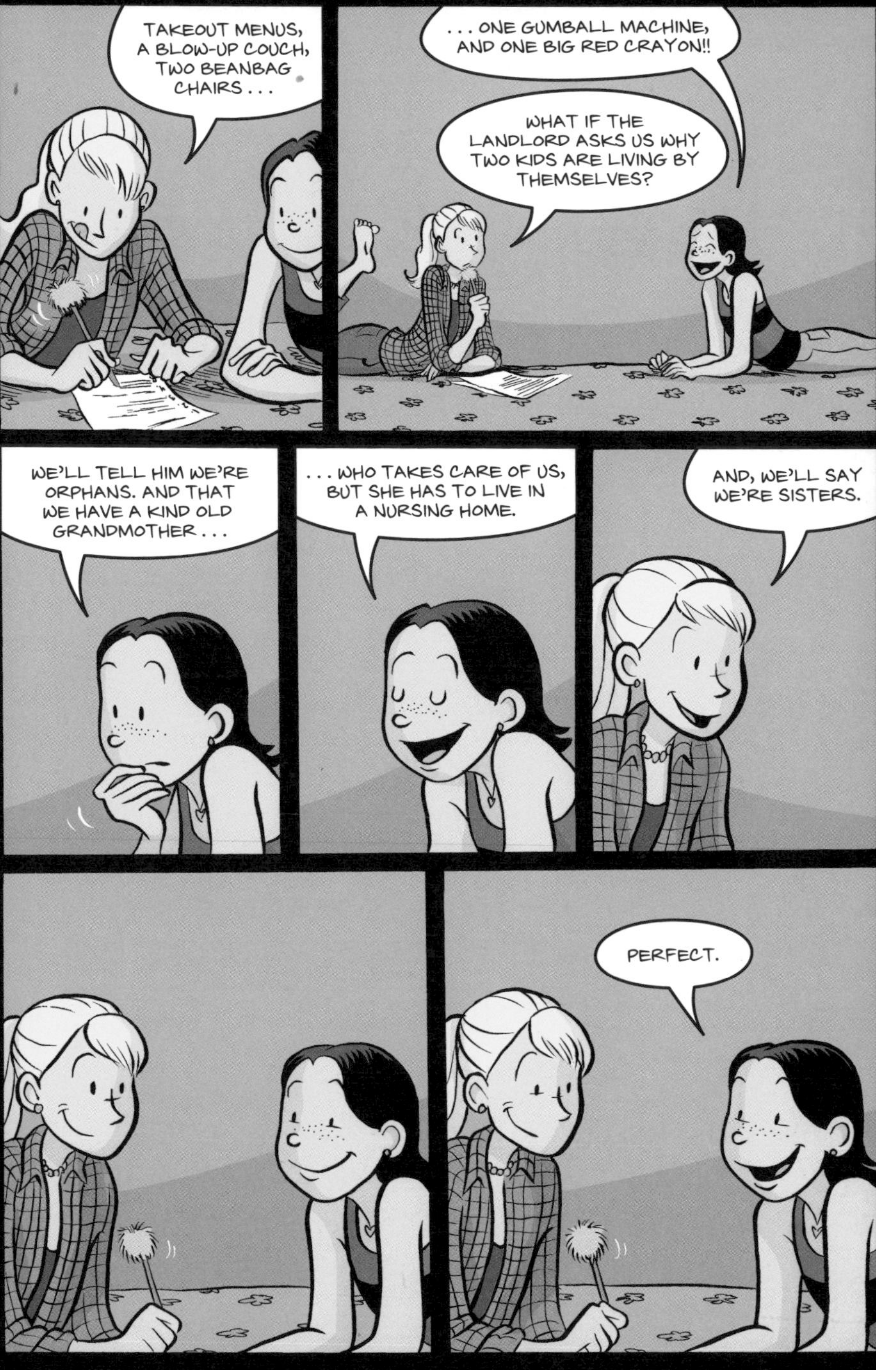
TAKEOUT MENUS, A BLOW-UP COUCH, TWO BEANBAG CHAIRS . . .
. . . ONE GUMBALL MACHINE, AND ONE BIG RED CRAYON!!
WHAT IF THE LANDLORD ASKS US WHY TWO KIDS ARE LIVING BY THEMSELVES?
WE'LL TELL HIM WE'RE ORPHANS. AND THAT WE HAVE A KIND OLD GRANDMOTHER . . .
. . . WHO TAKES CARE OF US, BUT SHE HAS TO LIVE IN A NURSING HOME.
AND, WE'LL SAY WE'RE SISTERS.
PERFECT.

OH, STACEY, YOU'RE HOME EARLY.

HOW WAS YOUR SITTING JOB?

IT WAS GOOD! CHARLOTTE'S SUCH A NEAT LITTLE KID.

Crunch

THAT'S NICE. YOU ALWAYS **DID** WANT A SISTER. I REMEMBER WHEN YOU AND LAINE USED TO--

USED TO WHAT? I WOULD **NEVER** WANT LAINE FOR A SISTER.

I DON'T EVEN WANT LAINE AS A FRIEND.

SIGH.

CHAPTER 8

KRISTY HAD A SURPRISE FOR US ON MONDAY MORNING WHEN WE GOT BACK TO SCHOOL.

YOU HAVE **GOT** TO BE KIDDING US!

WHAT?

OH, KRISTY, ARE YOU SERIOUS?!

COME ON, YOU GUYS! PUT THEM ON.

Join the BEST CLUB AROUND!

Join the BEST CLUB AROUND!

The
[B] ABY-
[S] ITTERS
[C] LUB

UM, GUYS?...

SCHOOL BUS

VROOOOMN...

Join the BEST CLUB AROUND!

Join the BEST CLUB ARO

Join the BEST CLUB

65

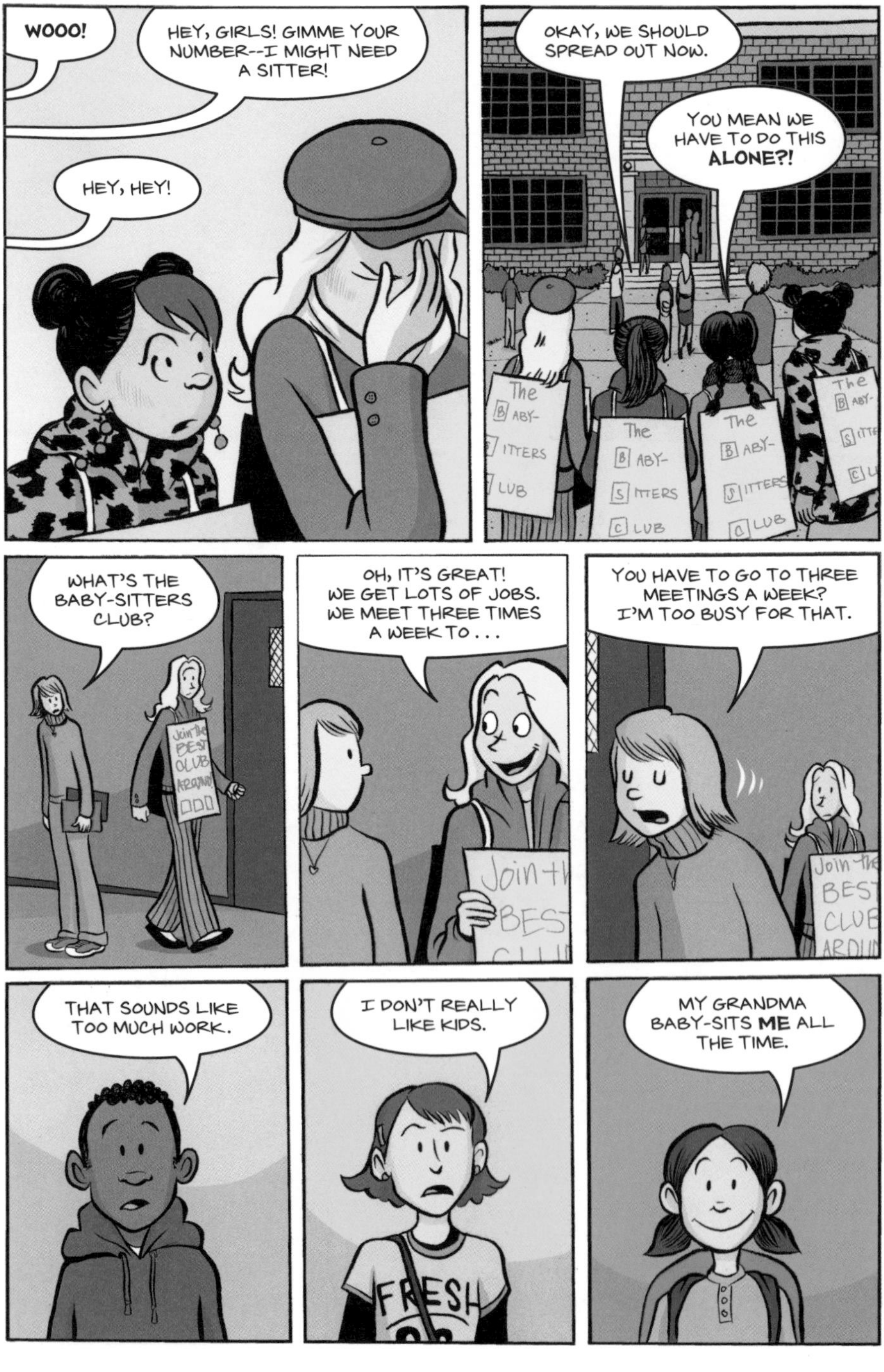
WOOO!
HEY, GIRLS! GIMME YOUR NUMBER--I MIGHT NEED A SITTER!
HEY, HEY!
OKAY, WE SHOULD SPREAD OUT NOW.
YOU MEAN WE HAVE TO DO THIS **ALONE?!**
The Baby-sitters Club
WHAT'S THE BABY-SITTERS CLUB?
Join the BEST CLUB AROUND
OH, IT'S GREAT! WE GET LOTS OF JOBS. WE MEET THREE TIMES A WEEK TO . . .
YOU HAVE TO GO TO THREE MEETINGS A WEEK? I'M TOO BUSY FOR THAT.
THAT SOUNDS LIKE TOO MUCH WORK.
I DON'T REALLY LIKE KIDS.
FRESH
MY GRANDMA BABY-SITS **ME** ALL THE TIME.

. . . STACEY?

OH . . . HEY, PETE!

AAAAAAAAAHH!!!

UM . . .

I WANTED TO ASK YOU . . .

OH, NO, OH, NO . . .

UH . . . DO YOU WANT TO GO TO THE SNOWFLAKE DANCE WITH ME??

--WHAT?

I . . . I MEAN, SURE! WOW! REALLY?! OKAY!

. . . GREAT! I'LL SEE YOU AT LUNCHTIME, OKAY?

AFTER THAT . . . WEARING THE SANDWICH BOARD WASN'T A BIG DEAL AT ALL!

LATER . . .

WHAT ARE **YOU** SO HAPPY ABOUT, KRISTY? NOBODY WANTS TO JOIN OUR CLUB!

YEAH . . .

I GOT TWO NEW MEMBERS. AND THEY'RE BOTH EIGHTH GRADERS.

REALLY?!

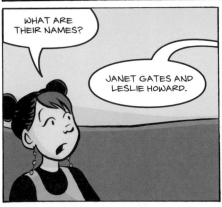

WHAT ARE THEIR NAMES?

JANET GATES AND LESLIE HOWARD.

. . . I THOUGHT THEY WERE FRIENDS OF LIZ'S?

NOT ANYMORE! THEY WERE PART OF THE AGENCY, BUT THEY DROPPED OUT. THEY DIDN'T LIKE IT.

GOSH.

AND THEY'RE COMING TO OUR NEXT MEETING!

CRUNCH CRUNCH

BUT . . . SOMETHING'S WRONG ABOUT THIS. SOMETHING . . . YES, I KNOW WHAT IT IS.

REMEMBER WHEN WE WERE FIRST STARTING THE CLUB, WE ASKED STACEY ALL SORTS OF QUESTIONS ABOUT THE BABY-SITTING SHE DID IN NEW YORK? WE DIDN'T KNOW HER, BUT WE KNEW THAT WE WANTED A CLUB OF GOOD BABY-SITTERS.

AND WE SAW RIGHT AWAY THAT STACEY WAS A GREAT SITTER . . . BUT DO YOU KNOW **ANYTHING** ABOUT JANET AND LESLIE, KRISTY?

WELL, NO . . .

AND YOU'VE ALREADY TOLD THEM THEY CAN BE MEMBERS?

YES . . .

THAT **DOES** SEEM RISKY.

WELL, IT'S TOO LATE NOW. WE'LL JUST HAVE TO TAKE OUR CHANCES.

ANYWAY . . . IF THE AGENCY IS AS HORRIBLE AS JANET AND LESLIE SAY, MAYBE IT WON'T LAST LONG.

I WONDER IF WE COULD MAKE IT RING IF WE ALL CONCENTRATED ON IT?

SIGH.

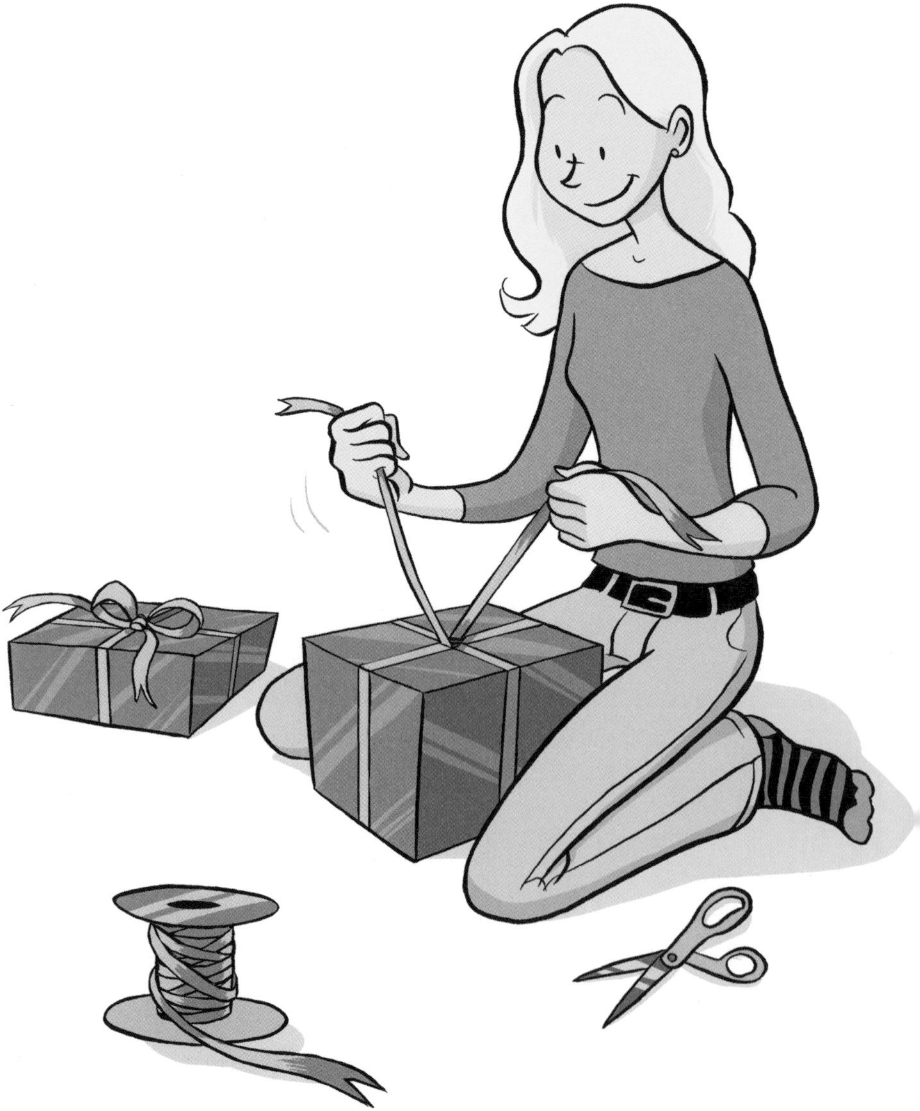

CHAPTER 9

THE NEXT AFTERNOON . . .

GIRLS! HELLO THERE! OH, I'M SO GLAD TO SEE YOU.

HI-HI!

HI, MRS. NEWTON!

COME IN, COME IN. JAMIE HAS MISSED YOU, AND I'M DYING FOR YOU TO MEET LUCY!

MOMMY? ARE ANY OF THOSE PRESENTS FOR ME?

JAMIE . . . IT'S NOT POLITE TO ASK.

YOU'RE IN LUCK, JAMIE . . . FOUR OF THESE PRESENTS ARE FOR YOU.

FOUR!!

I'M SORRY . . . IT'S BEEN A DIFFICULT WEEK. JAMIE HAS BEEN A BIT J-E-A-L-O-U-S. . . . LUCY HAS GOTTEN A LOT OF P-R-E-S-E-N-T-S.

LET'S GO PEEK AT THE BABY BEFORE I OPEN THE REST OF THE GIFTS YOU BROUGHT.

I WISH SHE WERE AWAKE SO YOU COULD HOLD HER, BUT SHE'S STILL NAPPING.

GASP!

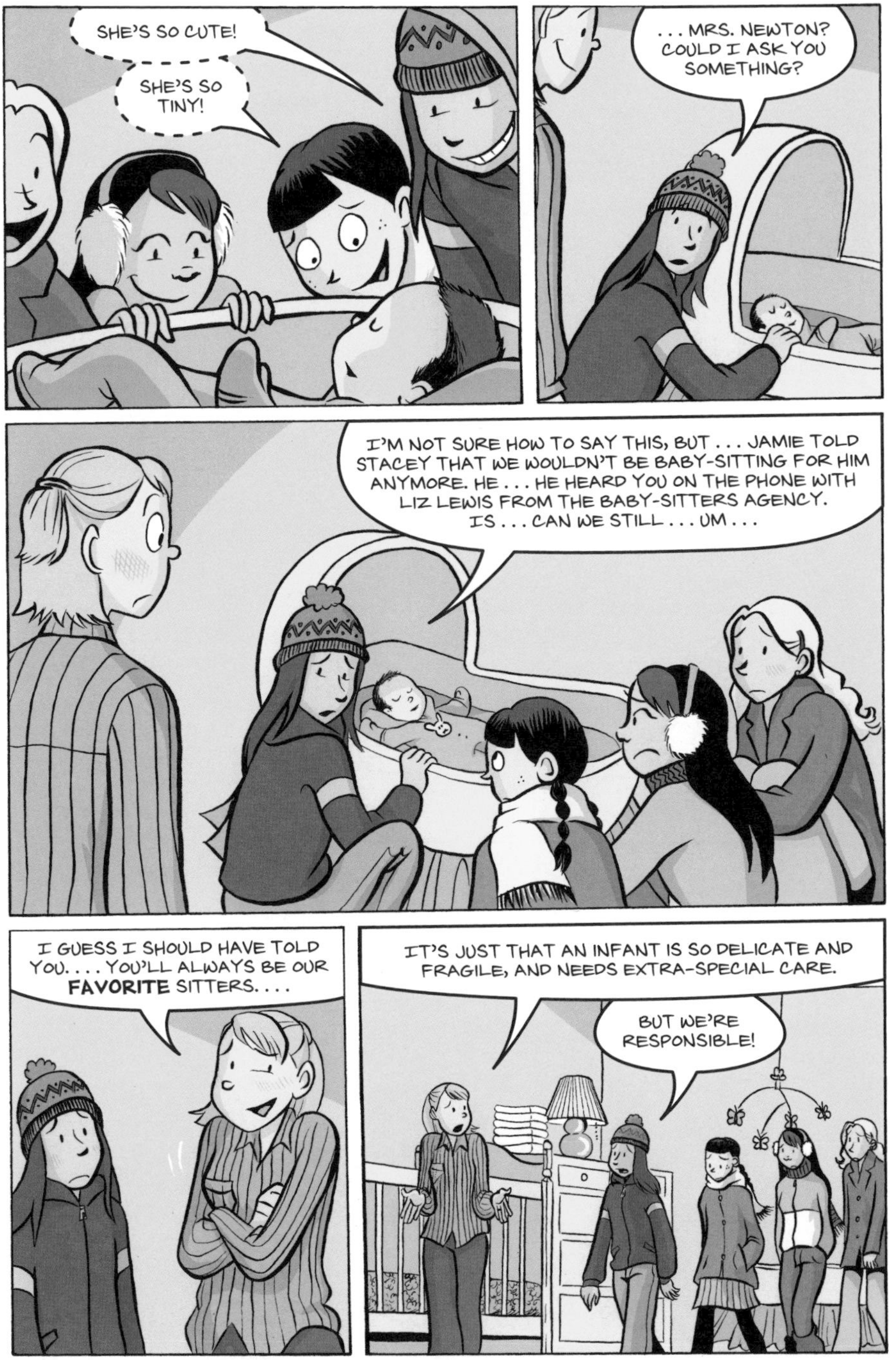
SHE'S SO CUTE!
SHE'S SO TINY!
. . . MRS. NEWTON? COULD I ASK YOU SOMETHING?
I'M NOT SURE HOW TO SAY THIS, BUT . . . JAMIE TOLD STACEY THAT WE WOULDN'T BE BABY-SITTING FOR HIM ANYMORE. HE . . . HE HEARD YOU ON THE PHONE WITH LIZ LEWIS FROM THE BABY-SITTERS AGENCY. IS . . . CAN WE STILL . . . UM . . .
I GUESS I SHOULD HAVE TOLD YOU. . . . YOU'LL ALWAYS BE OUR **FAVORITE** SITTERS. . . .
IT'S JUST THAT AN INFANT IS SO DELICATE AND FRAGILE, AND NEEDS EXTRA-SPECIAL CARE.
BUT WE'RE RESPONSIBLE!

I KNOW YOU ARE, BUT FOR THE NEXT FEW MONTHS, I'LL SIMPLY FEEL MORE COMFORTABLE LEAVING LUCY WITH AN OLDER SITTER.

. . . OKAY.

THE TIMES I TAKE LUCY WITH ME AND THERE'S JUST JAMIE TO SIT FOR, I'LL BE GLAD TO CALL THE BABY-SITTERS CLUB.

'BYE, KRISTY!

AND WHEN LUCY IS OLDER, I HOPE YOU'LL BE MY REGULAR SITTERS AGAIN!

SURE!

DEFINITELY.

OF COURSE.

YEAH.

. . . WE'RE DOOMED.

WEDNESDAY'S MEETING:

SO... HAVE YOU DONE A LOT OF BABY-SITTING?

TONS.

Snap Crack

YOU, TOO?

SURE.

WHERE?

ON THE OTHER SIDE OF TOWN. YOU PROBABLY WOULDN'T KNOW ANY OF THE PEOPLE.

TELL THEM HOW LATE YOU CAN STAY OUT.

MIDNIGHT.

I CAN STAY OUT TILL ANY TIME ON WEEKENDS, AS LONG AS I TELL MY MOM FIRST.

WHOA!

HOW OLD **ARE** YOU?

Snap
Snap
Chew

FOURTEEN.

I'M THIRTEEN.

RINNG

THE PHONE! OH MY GOSH! HELLO, BABY-SITTERS CLUB!

IT'S A NEW CLIENT--THE KELLYS. DO YOU WANT THE JOB, LESLIE?

WHY NOT.

RINNNNNG!!!

DO ONE OF YOU GUYS WANT TO ANSWER THAT?

...NOT REALLY.

GOOD AFTERNOON, BABY-SITTERS CLUB.... SURE! OKAY, WE'LL CALL YOU RIGHT BACK.

ANOTHER NEW CLIENT!! WOW. MRS. JAYDELL. SHE'S GOT TWO LITTLE KIDS. IT'S FOR SATURDAY NIGHT.... JANET, DO YOU WANT TO TAKE THIS ONE?

...HUH? OH, I GUESS.

HELLO, MRS. JAYDELL?...

THIS IS GOOD... THIS IS REALLY GOOD.

I'M SO RELIEVED!

IT SEEMED THE BABY-SITTERS CLUB WAS BACK ON TRACK.

RING!

WE HAD NO IDEA HOW WRONG WE WERE.

Monday, December 8

Today Kristy, Stacey + Mary Anne all
arived early for our baby-sitters club
meeting. We were all realy excited to find
out how Janet and Leslie's siting jobs
had gone on ~~800~~ Saturday.
   When it was 5:30 we kept expecting the
doorbell to ring any seconde. But it
didnt. Soon it was 5:50. Where were
they. Krist was getting worried. ~~Wed~~ Write
this down in our notebook, somebody,
she said. Somethings wrong.

                    * Claudia *

CHAPTER 10

OUR NEXT MEETING WAS THE FOLLOWING MONDAY.

BABY-SITTERS CLUB. OH, HI, MRS. MARSHALL! SURE!

CAN SOMEONE WATCH NINA AND ELEANOR ON WEDNESDAY AFTERNOON?

I'LL CHECK.

HEY...

...IT'S AFTER 5:30. SHOULDN'T JANET AND LESLIE BE HERE BY NOW??

HMM, YEAH...

RING!

BABY-SITTERS CLUB... MRS. NEWTON!! HI!

FOR JUST JAMIE? OF COURSE!

RING!

BABY-SI-- OH, HI, WATSON! YEAH, I'D LOVE TO SIT FOR KAREN AND ANDREW! LET ME SEE IF I'M FREE THEN...

UM... YOU GUYS?

5:50

THEY COULD HAVE AT LEAST CALLED TO SAY THEY WEREN'T GOING TO MAKE TODAY'S MEETING . . .

I SAW JANET IN SCHOOL TODAY, AND SHE DIDN'T SAY ANYTHING ABOUT NOT COMING.

WELL, I'LL CALL THEM TO SEE IF--

RING!

HELLO, BABY-SITTERS CLUB. YES, THIS IS KRISTY THOMAS, CLUB PRESIDENT... OH, HELLO, MR. KELLY...

SHE **DIDN'T**?!

I'M SO SORRY. I DIDN'T KNOW. WELL, SHE ISN'T HERE RIGHT NOW.... I FEEL TERRIBLE.

click

LESLIE NEVER SHOWED UP FOR HER JOB AT THE KELLYS' ON SATURDAY.

WHAT?! WHY DIDN'T THE KELLYS CALL US ON SATURDAY?

SIMPLE! LESLIE SHOWED THEM WE WEREN'T TRUSTWORTHY! MR. KELLY WAS ONLY CALLING NOW TO MAKE SURE WE KNEW ABOUT IT . . . BUT I HAVE A FEELING THE KELLYS WON'T BE CALLING THE BABY-SITTERS CLUB AGAIN.

RING!

HELLO, BABY-SITTERS CLUB. YES? . . . OH, NO, YOU'RE **KIDDING.**

IT'S MRS. JAYDELL.

MRS. JAYDELL? DID JANET NOT SHOW UP FOR HER JOB?

GRAB

NO, WE HAD NO IDEA. I'M SORRY YOU MISSED THE COCKTAIL PARTY . . . YES . . . I UNDERSTAND.

click!

AAAAAAAAAHH!!

THE NEXT DAY...

WE ARE GOING TO TEACH THOSE TRAITORS A **LESSON.**

YOU'RE SURE THEY FLAKED OUT ON THEIR JOBS ON PURPOSE??

POSITIVE.

THEIR HOMEROOMS ARE BOTH IN THIS HALL. SO WE'LL WAIT FOR THEM HERE.

... I SEE THEM! AND THEY'RE WITH ...

... LIZ LEWIS!!

I THOUGHT THEY DIDN'T LIKE LIZ!

I KNOW.

OKAY, WHAT IS GOING ON? WHERE WERE YOU YESTERDAY??

Snicker

HA HA HA
HA HAHH!!

WHAT'S SO
FUNNY?

WE . . . ARE MEMBERS OF THE
BABY-SITTERS **AGENCY.**

BUT--
BUT--

HAHA
HAAAA!!

WE HAD YOU
COMPLETELY
FOOLED!!

THIS IS ROTTEN. I'M GOING TO
TELL ALL THE PARENTS WE SIT
FOR THAT YOU . . .

SO YOU'RE GOING TO
TATTLE ON US? YOU
WOULDN'T DARE.

LIZ AND MICHELLE WILL JUST HAVE TO WORK A LITTLE HARDER TO BE THE BEST SITTING AGENCY IN TOWN. LATER!

I'M SO EMBARRASSED! I SHOULD HAVE CHECKED ON THEM FIRST.

IT'S OKAY, KRISTY.

WE'LL JUST HAVE TO KEEP GOING. THE FOUR OF US. SO WHAT IF WE'RE ONLY TWELVE? SO WHAT IF WE CAN'T STAY OUT LATE?

YEAH!

I THINK **WE'RE** THE BETTER BABY-SITTING SERVICE. . . . WE JUST HAVE TO THINK OF A WAY TO PROVE IT!

Wednesday, December 10th

Earlier this afternoon, I baby-sat for Jamie
while Mrs. Newton took Lucy to a doctor's
appointment. Something was bothering him. He
moped around as if he'd lost his best friend.
He greeted me cheerfully enough when I
arrived, but as soon as Mrs. Newton carried
a bundled-up Lucy out the back door, his
face fell....

                          Mary Anne

CHAPTER 11

IT MUST BE KIND OF TOUGH HAVING A NEW BABY AT YOUR HOUSE, HUH, JAMIE?

IT'S OKAY.

DOES SHE CRY A LOT?

NOT MUCH. MOMMY ROCKS HER, SHE STOPS.

YOU SEEM KIND OF SAD.

BABY-SITTERS USED TO BE FUN.

THEY USED TO PLAY GAMES WITH ME, AND COLOR MONSTER PICTURES, AND READ ME STORIES.

. . . AND NOW THEY'RE TOO BUSY TAKING CARE OF THE BABY?

NO. . .

TOO BUSY WATCHING TV. ARE **YOU** GOING TO WATCH TV, MARY ANNE?

ME? NO, I WAS GOING TO ASK IF YOU WANTED TO SEE WHAT'S IN THE KID-KIT TODAY.

THE KID-KIT!! YOU BROUGHT IT? I DIDN'T SEE!

IT'S IN THE FRONT HALL. BUT WAIT A SECOND, JAMIE...

Leap!

TELL ME MORE ABOUT YOUR BABY-SITTERS. ARE YOU SAYING ALL THEY DO IS WATCH TV?

AND THEY... THEY HAVE **ACCIDENTS.**

WHAT KIND OF "ACCIDENTS"?

LIKE THIS.

...A BURN MARK!

HI, STACEY. I'M GLAD YOU'RE HERE.... CHARLOTTE HAS BEEN IN A FUNNY MOOD LATELY.

SHE SAYS SHE FEELS FINE, BUT SHE'S BEEN VERY OUT OF SORTS. I'VE ARRANGED A CONFERENCE WITH HER TEACHER.

BUT I JUST WANTED YOU TO KNOW.

MR. JOHANSSEN IS WORKING LATE TONIGHT, AND I HAVE A P.T.A. MEETING. WE'LL BOTH BE BACK BEFORE 9:00.

OKAY.

WHEN YOU COME HOME, COULD I TALK TO YOU? WE'RE LEAVING FOR NEW YORK ON SATURDAY, AND I HAVE AN IDEA.

CERTAINLY.

SEE YOU LATER, SWEETIE.

MMM.

SO! DO YOU NEED ANY HELP WITH YOUR HOMEWORK, CHARLOTTE?

NO, IT'S EASY.

WELL, IF IT'S EASY, YOU'LL BE FINISHED SOON, RIGHT?

WHAT DO YOU CARE?!

CHARLOTTE! WHY ARE YOU TALKING TO ME LIKE THAT? WHY ARE YOU MAD?

I'M NOT MAD.

YOU **SOUND** MAD. I ONLY ASKED BECAUSE I WANT TO READ "THE CRICKET IN TIMES SQUARE" WITH YOU WHEN YOU'RE DONE.

OH, **SURE.**

YOUR MOTHER SAID YOU **WANTED** ME TO SIT FOR YOU!

I WANTED YOU TO COME OVER.... I DIDN'T WANT YOU TO BABY-SIT.

I DON'T THINK I UNDERSTAND.

STACEY, HOW COME YOU BABY-SIT FOR ME?

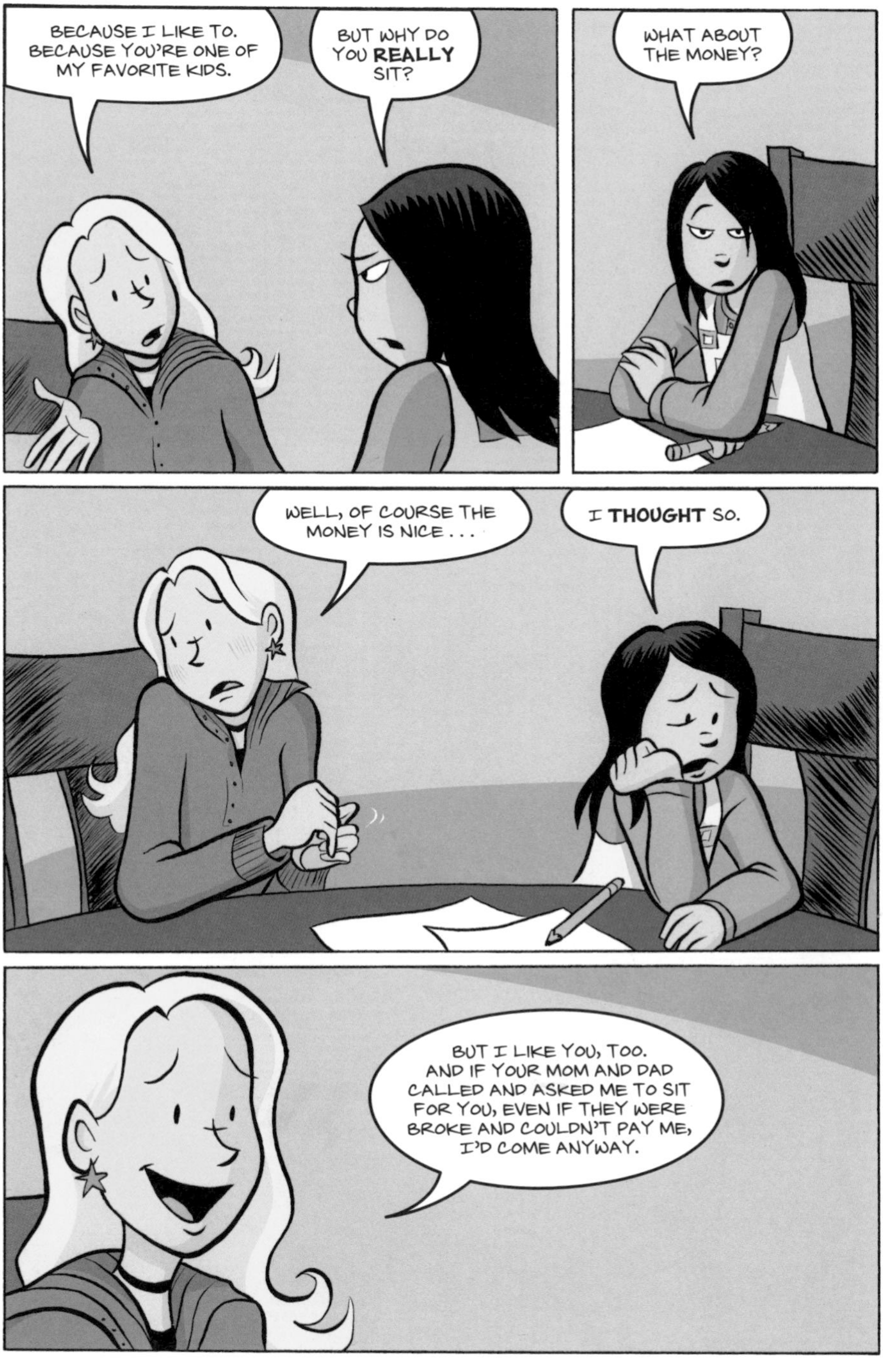
BECAUSE I LIKE TO. BECAUSE YOU'RE ONE OF MY FAVORITE KIDS.
BUT WHY DO YOU **REALLY** SIT?
WHAT ABOUT THE MONEY?
WELL, OF COURSE THE MONEY IS NICE . . .
I **THOUGHT** SO.
BUT I LIKE YOU, TOO. AND IF YOUR MOM AND DAD CALLED AND ASKED ME TO SIT FOR YOU, EVEN IF THEY WERE BROKE AND COULDN'T PAY ME, I'D COME ANYWAY.

SOME BABY-SITTERS ONLY SIT BECAUSE THEY WANT MONEY... THEY DON'T CARE ABOUT THE KIDS.

WHICH BABY-SITTERS?

... MY NEW ONES.

WHO ARE YOUR NEW ONES?

MICHELLE PATTERSON. LESLIE SOMEBODY. AND CATHY MORRIS.

AND THEY **TOLD** YOU THEY DON'T LIKE SITTING FOR YOU?!

NO, CATHY'S SISTER ELLIE TOLD ME. SHE'S IN MY CLASS. SHE HATES ME.

ELLIE SAID, "OH, CHARLOTTE, TEACHER'S PET, YOU DON'T HAVE ANY FRIENDS!" AND I SAID, "I HAVE BABY-SITTERS. **THEY'RE** MY FRIENDS." AND ELLIE SAID, "MY SISTER CATHY ONLY SITS FOR YOU BECAUSE YOUR PARENTS PAY HER A LOT OF MONEY, STUPID."

HEY, CHAR . . . I INVITED YOU TO JAMIE NEWTON'S BIG BROTHER PARTY, DIDN'T I? I WASN'T SITTING FOR YOU THEN.

SNIFF YEAH . . .

AND WHAT DO MICHELLE AND LESLIE AND CATHY DO WHEN THEY BABY-SIT FOR YOU?

WATCH TV. TALK ON THE PHONE. ONCE LESLIE BROUGHT HER BOYFRIEND OVER.

WHAT DO I DO WHEN I BABY-SIT?

WELL, YOU BRING THE KID-KIT. WE READ STORIES, AND TAKE WALKS, AND PLAY GAMES. . . .

THAT'S BEING A FRIEND, ISN'T IT?

...YES!!

I'M SORRY, STACEY. I'M SORRY I WAS ANGRY.

DO YOU WANT TO TALK TO ME ABOUT THOSE KIDS AT YOUR SCHOOL? THE ONES WHO WERE TEASING YOU?

NO.

WELL, IF YOU EVER NEED TO TALK ABOUT IT, YOU CAN ALWAYS TALK TO ME!

LATER...

SO, STACEY, WHAT DID YOU WANT TO TALK TO ME ABOUT?

WELL, I FIGURE I'LL LET MOM AND DAD TAKE ME TO THEIR "DOCTOR" ON SATURDAY...

BUT I ALSO WANT TO TELL THEM I'VE BEEN RESEARCHING DIABETES ON MY OWN, AND TELL THEM ABOUT A DOCTOR **I'VE** CHOSEN WHO I WANT TO SEE. WHICH IS WHERE YOU COME IN.

I WAS HOPING YOU COULD RECOMMEND SOMEONE SENSIBLE . . . AND PREFERABLY, SOMEONE WITH A FANCY OFFICE AND LOTS OF DIPLOMAS.

WELL, I WAS ACTUALLY ABOUT TO **GIVE** YOU A RECOMMENDATION. WE MUST'VE BEEN THINKING ALONG THE SAME LINES.

IF I PULL A FEW STRINGS, I SHOULD BE ABLE TO GET YOU AN APPOINTMENT FOR SATURDAY.

OH, THANK YOU!!!

BUT I'D RATHER EXPLAIN THINGS TO YOUR PARENTS.

OH, NO, PLEASE DON'T!! IT HAS TO BE A SURPRISE . . . OTHERWISE IT'LL **NEVER** WORK.

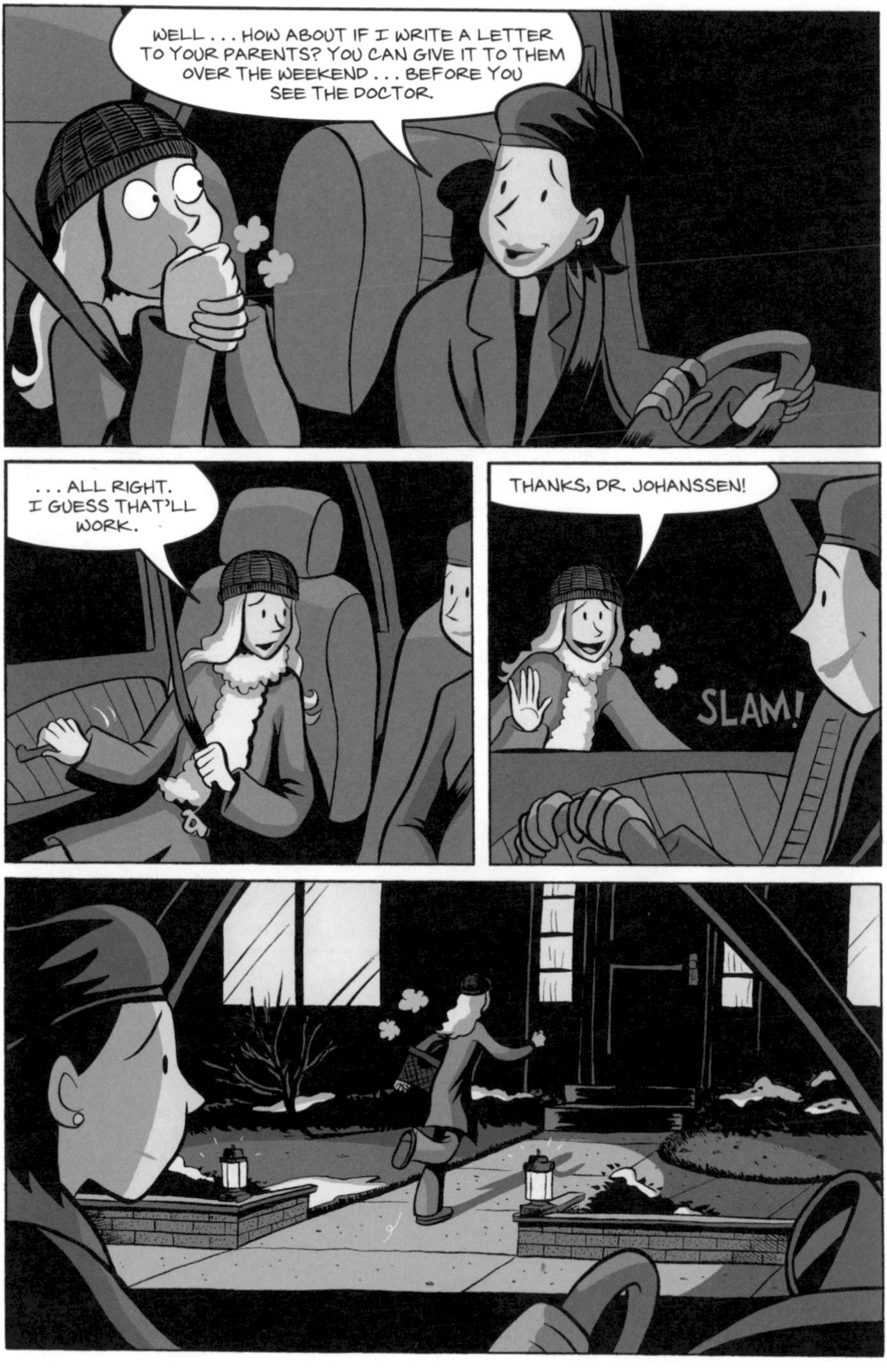
WELL . . . HOW ABOUT IF I WRITE A LETTER TO YOUR PARENTS? YOU CAN GIVE IT TO THEM OVER THE WEEKEND . . . BEFORE YOU SEE THE DOCTOR.
. . . ALL RIGHT. I GUESS THAT'LL WORK.
THANKS, DR. JOHANSSEN!
SLAM!

CHAPTER 12

WE'VE GOT A PROBLEM.

AFTER SCHOOL THE NEXT DAY, MARY ANNE AND I TOLD KRISTY AND CLAUDIA WHAT WE'D LEARNED FROM JAMIE AND CHARLOTTE.

ANOTHER ONE?

WHEN I SAT FOR CHARLOTTE LAST NIGHT, SHE WAS **REALLY** UPSET ABOUT HER NEW SITTERS.

OH, JAMIE WAS UPSET ABOUT **HIS,** TOO! BUT IT MIGHT END UP WORKING IN OUR FAVOR.

WHAT? HOW?!

WELL, I TOLD JAMIE TO TELL HIS MOTHER HE WAS UNHAPPY. WE CAN'T SAY ANYTHING TO THE PARENTS . . . BUT THE KIDS WE SIT FOR CAN!

THAT'S TRUE!

MAYBE FROM NOW ON, WE SHOULD ENCOURAGE THE KIDS TO SPEAK UP... THEY HAVE THE RIGHT.

AND WE **HAVE** TO REMIND OURSELVES THAT WE'RE QUALITY SITTERS, WHO...

HI-HI!

JAMIE!!

WHAT ARE YOU DOING HERE?

PLAYING.

WELL, YOU SHOULDN'T BE IN THE STREET. AND WHERE ARE YOUR MITTENS? AND YOUR HAT? IT'S **FREEZING** OUT HERE!

IS YOUR MOTHER VERY BUSY WITH LUCY TODAY?

NO, SHE'S AT A MEETING. LUCY'S ASLEEP.

ZZZZZZZMMMM

SPLASH!

JAMIE, DO YOU HAVE A BABY-SITTER TODAY?

YEAH, BARB-- ...NO, CATHY.

CATHY MORRIS?

YEAH.

DOES SHE KNOW YOU'RE OUT HERE?

SHE SAID I COULD PLAY OUTSIDE.

shrug

WHAT SHOULD WE DO?

JAMIE, CAN YOU DO TWO SPECIAL THINGS? JUST FOR US?

YES.

FIRST GO FIND YOUR HAT AND MITTENS. ASK CATHY FOR HELP IF YOU CAN'T FIND THEM. BUT DON'T GO OUTDOORS WITHOUT THEM, OKAY?

YES.

SECOND, PLAY OUT BACK IF YOU WANT TO BE OUTDOORS. PLAY ON YOUR SWING, OKAY?

OKAY.

WOW. THIS IS SERIOUS. THAT BABY-SITTER, WHOEVER THE SO-CALLED AGENCY FOUND, LETS THREE-YEAR-OLDS PLAY OUTSIDE ON THEIR OWN.

HE COULD'VE BEEN HIT BY A CAR.

HE COULD'VE WANDERED OFF.

THE BROOK'S NOT FROZEN OVER YET. WHAT IF HE FELL IN?!

WE **HAVE** TO DO SOMETHING. I THINK WE SHOULD TELL MRS. NEWTON.

BUT WHAT IF SHE THINKS WE'RE POOR SPORTS?

I THINK JAMIE'S SAFETY IS WORTH US RISKING LOOKING LIKE POOR SPORTS.

I THINK SO, TOO.

ME, TOO.

IT'S JUST THAT. . .

THERE'S MRS. NEWTON'S CAR. NOW'S OUR CHANCE.

WAIT, CATHY'S STILL INSIDE. . . . WE CAN'T GO IN **YET.**

WELL, THEN . . . WE'LL WAIT.

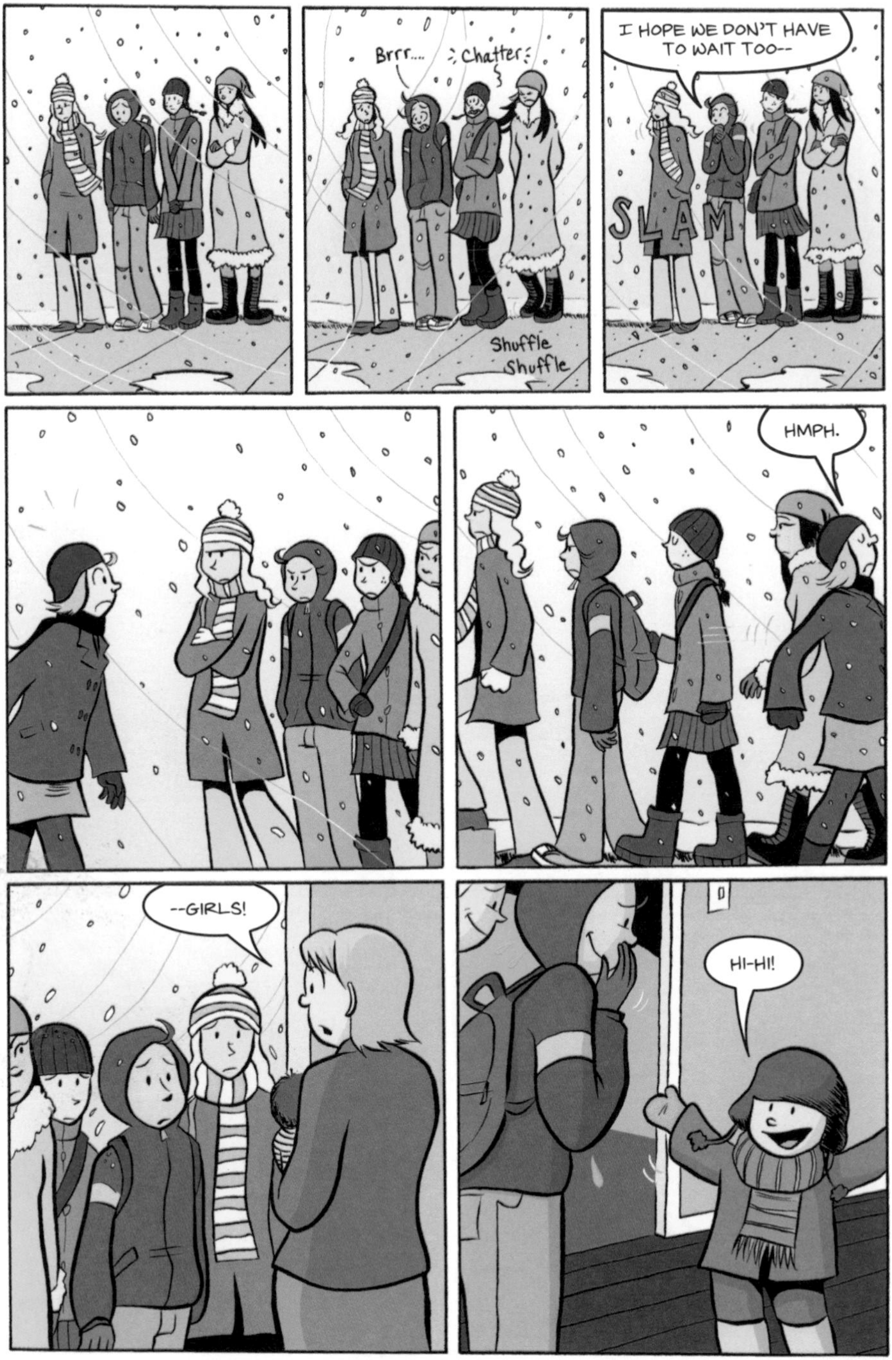
Brrr....
Chatter
Shuffle
Shuffle
I HOPE WE DON'T HAVE TO WAIT TOO--
SLAM
HMPH.
--GIRLS!
HI-HI!

I DID WHAT YOU SAID!!

COULD WE TALK TO YOU ALONE?

O-OF COURSE... IS SOMETHING WRONG?

I GUESS WE SHOULD BEGIN WITH WHAT HAPPENED THIS AFTERNOON.

WE WERE WALKING HOME FROM SCHOOL, AND WE SAW JAMIE PLAYING OUTSIDE.

BY HIMSELF.

IN THE STREET.

WITH NO HAT OR MITTENS.

HE TOLD US CATHY MORRIS WAS BABY-SITTING FOR HIM, BUT SHE WAS NOWHERE TO BE SEEN... WE DON'T THINK SHE KNEW WHERE JAMIE WAS.

WE FELT YOU REALLY OUGHT TO KNOW.

!

WE'RE SORRY TO BE SUCH TATTLETALES, BUT WE--

NO, NO!

I'M GLAD YOU TOLD ME. I'M JUST--I CAN'T BELIEVE-- THAT WAS SO **IRRESPONSIBLE** OF HER.

JAMIE ALSO TOLD MARY ANNE THAT HE HASN'T LIKED HIS NEW SITTERS.

ONE OF THE SITTERS SMOKES, AND BURNED A HOLE IN THE CHAIR YOU'RE SITTING ON.

OH.

CHARLOTTE JOHANSSEN HAS BEEN UPSET, TOO. WE HAD A LONG TALK ABOUT IT LAST NIGHT.

WELL . . .

I CERTAINLY WON'T USE THE AGENCY ANYMORE, ALTHOUGH WE DID FIND ONE 17-YEAR-OLD WE LIKE VERY MUCH.

I'LL CONTINUE TO CALL HIM ON HIS OWN. . . . I ADMIT JAMIE HASN'T SEEMED HAPPY LATELY, BUT I BLAMED IT ON SIBLING RIVALRY.

ANYWAY, I'LL PHONE DR. JOHANSSEN, AND A FEW OTHER PARENTS--THEY'LL WANT TO KNOW WHAT YOU TOLD ME.

AND I'LL CALL LIZ AND MICHELLE, BOTH OF THEM. AND CATHY MORRIS, OF COURSE.

I WISH I KNEW WHICH ONE WAS THE SMOKER.

MRS. NEWTON, I KNOW YOU WANT TO CALL CATHY ABOUT THIS AFTERNOON YOURSELF. . .

. . . BUT COULD YOU LET **US** TALK TO LIZ AND MICHELLE OURSELVES?

CHAPTER 13

OH, LIKE, LOOK WHO IT IS. THE BABY CLUB.

LIKE, HA HA.

WHAT, SO YOUR LITTLE CLUB FAILED, AND NOW YOU WANT TO COME WORK FOR US?

NO WAY. WE'RE HERE TO TALK ABOUT AN IMPORTANT BUSINESS MATTER.

AND WHAT IS SO IMPORTANT?

YESTERDAY CATHY MORRIS WAS SITTING FOR A THREE-YEAR-OLD, AND SHE LET HIM GO OUTDOORS BY HIMSELF.

SO?

SO?! WE FOUND HIM PLAYING **IN THE STREET** BY HIMSELF! THREE-YEAR-OLDS CANNOT PLAY OUTSIDE BY THEMSELVES--GOOD BABY-SITTERS OUGHT TO KNOW THAT.

FINE. WE WON'T GIVE CATHY ANY MORE JOBS.

SHE DOESN'T REALLY LIKE BABY-SITTING ANYWAY.

SHRUG

WE, ON THE OTHER HAND, LIKE BABY-SITTING JUST FINE.

WHY, 'CAUSE YOU CAN TALK ON THE PHONE OR WATCH TV THE WHOLE TIME YOU'RE SITTING?

WHOA, WHOA. WE PAY ATTENTION TO THE KIDS WE SIT FOR.

FINE, WHAT'S JAMIE NEWTON'S FAVORITE KIND OF SANDWICH?

I ONLY SAT FOR HIM ONCE.

IT'S PEANUT BUTTER AND HONEY, TOASTED.

DO YOU KNOW CHARLOTTE JOHANSSEN'S FAVORITE GAME?

... CANDYLAND?

CHARLOTTE'S REALLY SMART! HER FAVORITE GAME IS SCRABBLE!

DO YOU KNOW WHAT NINA MARSHALL IS ALLERGIC TO?

WHAT IS THIS, TWENTY QUESTIONS?

COME ON. IF YOU'VE EVER SAT FOR NINA, YOU SHOULD KNOW.

I'LL GIVE YOU A HINT. IT'S A FOOD. WHAT FOOD WOULD MAKE HER BREAK OUT IN HIVES IF SHE ATE IT?

I DON'T KNOW, OKAY?

STRAWBERRIES.

WHAT ARE YOU TRYING TO PROVE, THAT YOU'RE BETTER BABY-SITTERS THAN WE ARE?

YOU SAID IT, NOT ME.

OKAY, SO YOU PROVED IT. NOW GO AWAY AND LEAVE US ALONE.

THAT AFTERNOON . . .

EXIT ¼ MI

SO, WHO'RE WE STAYING WITH THIS TIME--AUNT BEV AND UNCLE LOU, OR AUNTIE CARLA AND UNCLE ERIC?

WE'RE NOT STAYING WITH EITHER OF THEM.

GASP YOU MEAN WE'RE STAYING IN A HOTEL?!

NO. . .

WE'RE STAYING WITH THE CUMMINGSES. YOU CAN SEE LAINE AGAIN!

WHAT?!
THE CUMMINGSES??

DO THEY KNOW WHAT'S WRONG WITH ME, THEN? HAVE YOU FINALLY TOLD THEM ABOUT MY DIABETES?

YES, WE FINALLY TOLD THEM. LAINE KNOWS, TOO.

HOW COULD YOU DO THIS TO ME?! YOU KNOW LAINE HATES ME. AND I HATE HER.

OH, STACEY. THAT WAS MONTHS AGO. I'M SURE YOU AND LAINE ARE OVER THAT FIGHT!

HI.

HMPH!

I JUST WANT YOU TO KNOW THAT I'M NOT ANY HAPPIER ABOUT THIS THAN YOU ARE. I WANTED TO STAY IN A HOTEL.

STACEY--

SLAM!

THAT NIGHT, I NOTICED LAINE WATCHING ME VERY CAREFULLY.

BUT THERE WASN'T MUCH FOR HER TO SEE.

I DON'T KNOW WHAT SHE WAS EXPECTING. NOBODY GAVE ME ANY SPECIAL ATTENTION, FOOD, OR FAVORS.

THE NEXT MORNING . . .

MR. AND MRS. MCGILL? DR. BARNES WILL MEET WITH YOU IN A FEW MINUTES. STACEY, PLEASE COME WITH ME.

?!

WE'LL SEE YOU AGAIN SOON, STACEY.

MOM? DAD?

CAN WE GO NEXT DOOR AND GET SOMETHING TO DRINK?

YES, GOOD IDEA.

... AND THEN SHE MADE ME TAKE WHAT I **THINK** WAS AN I.Q. TEST. AND I HAVEN'T EVEN SEEN DR. BARNES YET! WHAT'S HE LIKE?

HE'S ... WELL ...

LISTEN, MOM, DAD ... I'VE BEEN THINKING. YOU GUYS WERE RIGHT. IT'S IMPORTANT TO LEARN ABOUT DIABETES, AND HOW TO LIVE WITH IT.

I'VE BEEN LOOKING INTO IT MYSELF.

YOU HAVE? GOOD FOR YOU.

YEAH, AND I ... I HEARD ABOUT THIS DOCTOR, DR. GRAHAM.

HE'S A BIG AUTHORITY ON CHILDHOOD DISEASES, ESPECIALLY DIABETES.

THE THING IS, I HAVE AN APPOINTMENT WITH HIM TODAY. IT'S SORT OF A SURPRISE.

THIS IS FROM CHARLOTTE'S MOTHER, DR. JOHANSSEN. I THINK YOU'D BETTER READ IT NOW.

WHAT? HONEY, I—

JUST **READ** IT.

THE LETTER EXPLAINED THAT I HAD GONE TO DR. JOHANSSEN CONFIDENTIALLY, WHICH WAS WHY SHE HADN'T CONTACTED MY PARENTS PERSONALLY.

IT ALSO PRAISED DR. GRAHAM'S WORK, AND APOLOGIZED TO MOM AND DAD FOR ANY INCONVENIENCE.

STACEY, I'M NOT QUITE SURE WHAT TO THINK OF ALL THIS.

I THOUGHT YOU'D BE PLEASED.

WE ARE, WE JUST... WE DON'T KNOW ANYTHING ABOUT HIM. WE DON'T KNOW HOW EXPENSIVE HE IS, OR . . .

I WISH YOU'D DISCUSSED THIS WITH US BEFORE YOU MADE AN APPOINTMENT.

YOU MAKE APPOINTMENTS FOR ME WITHOUT ASKING **ME** FIRST.

TRUE...

DR. GRAHAM... HIS NAME SOUNDS FAMILIAR.

YES.

HE'S SUPPOSED TO BE EXCELLENT, BUT VERY BUSY AND ALMOST IMPOSSIBLE TO SEE. YOU WERE LUCKY TO GET AN APPOINTMENT.

WELL, MY APPOINTMENT'S IN 15 MINUTES.... WE'D BETTER GET GOING IF WE WANT TO MAKE IT.

HELLO, YOU MUST BE STACEY. I'M DR. PHILIP GRAHAM.

HI!

WE'RE SORRY SHE SET UP THE APPOINTMENT WITHOUT...

IT'S NO PROBLEM. WON'T YOU HAVE A SEAT?

I'M NOT GOING TO EXAMINE STACEY TODAY... I JUST WANT TO ASK SOME QUESTIONS.

SOME QUESTIONS! HE ASKED A BILLION. ABOUT MY BIRTH, MY HEALTH BEFORE THE DIABETES WAS DISCOVERED, MY NEW SCHOOL, MY FRIENDS.

WE TALKED FOREVER, AND HE EVEN MADE MY PARENTS FEEL COMFORTABLE.

WELL... YOU MUST BE VERY PROUD OF YOUR DAUGHTER.

OH, YES, ABSOLUTELY.

FROM WHAT YOU'VE TOLD ME, STACEY WAS A VERY SICK YOUNG LADY, BUT SHE'S MADE EXCELLENT PROGRESS WITH HER TREATMENT.

I CAN ONLY SEE ONE PROBLEM.

WHAT'S THAT??

ALTHOUGH STACEY HAS TAKEN THE MOVE TO CONNECTICUT IN STRIDE, SHE SEEMS TO FEEL QUITE UNSETTLED ABOUT HER DISEASE.

SHE WANTS TO BE ABLE TO HAVE SOME CONTROL OVER IT, BUT SHE'S A LITTLE AFRAID OF IT. IS THAT RIGHT?

WELL . . .

I GUESS. EVERY TIME I THINK I UNDERSTAND IT, WE SEE SOME **OTHER** DOCTOR WHO SAYS SOMETHING DIFFERENT.

DR. JOHANSSEN SAID SHE THINKS DR. BARNES MIGHT MAKE ME GO TO A PSYCHIATRIST, OR EVEN CHANGE SCHOOLS.

BUT I DON'T **WANT** TO CHANGE SCHOOLS! I DON'T WANT TO SEE ANY MORE DOCTORS!

I MUST ADMIT. . . WE **WERE** A BIT PERPLEXED BY MANY OF THE TESTS DR. BARNES WAS PLANNING TO GIVE STACEY ON MONDAY AND TUESDAY.

WHAT DO **YOU** THINK OF DR. BARNES' CLINIC?

I THINK IT'S A LOT OF BUNK. NOTHING HE'LL DO WILL HARM STACEY, BUT I DON'T THINK ANY OF IT IS NECESSARY.

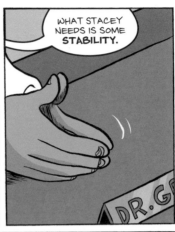

WHAT STACEY NEEDS IS SOME **STABILITY**.

DR. GR

SHE SEEMS INCREDIBLY HEALTHY, CONSIDERING HOW ILL SHE WAS A YEAR AGO.

AND SHE SEEMS TO HAVE A VERY GOOD HANDLE ON HER INSULIN INJECTIONS AND HER DIET.

MAYBE... IT'S TIME **STACEY** HAD MORE TO SAY ABOUT HER TREATMENTS.

DO YOU **WANT** TO GO BACK TO THE CLINIC?

NO!

THANK YOU, DR. GRAHAM.

OF COURSE! PLEASE CALL ME IF YOU HAVE ANY QUESTIONS.

CHAPTER 14

WHILE WE ATE DINNER, MOM AND DAD AND I TALKED ABOUT EVERYTHING. MOSTLY, HOW THEY HADN'T LIKED DR. BARNES ANYWAY.

AND THEN WE MET MR. AND MRS. CUMMINGS AND LAINE AT A MOVIE THEATER.

OH, IT'S CROWDED.... WE'LL SIT OVER THERE, AND LAINE AND STACEY CAN TAKE THOSE TWO SEATS IN THE BACK.

THANKS FOR ASKING IF **I** WANTED SOMETHING.

YOU CAN'T EAT ANY OF THIS STUFF ANYWAY.

I CAN EAT POPCORN. I CAN DRINK DIET SODA.

POP CORN

FREEZ

WELL, I DIDN'T KNOW!

IF YOU EVER BOTHERED TO SPEAK TO ME, YOU'D...

SHHH!!

YOFRE

YOU DON'T TALK TO ME EITHER. YOU NEVER EVEN TOLD ME THE TRUTH ABOUT YOUR...YOUR SICKNESS.

WHY WOULD I WANT TO TALK TO SOMEONE WHO TURNS ALL MY FRIENDS AGAINST....

SHHH!!

POP CORN

EXCUSE ME, LAINE. I'D LIKE TO GET MYSELF A SNACK.

A SMALL DIET COKE AND A SMALL POPCORN, NO BUTTER, PLEASE.

THAT'LL BE $9.25.

BEEP BEEP

OH...UM...I FORGOT HOW EXPENSIVE THINGS ARE IN NEW YORK....

THERE YOU GO.

...THANKS.

STACEY?

YEAH?

I'M SORRY.

YOU ARE?!

YEAH.

I'M SORRY, TOO. . . . I GUESS I SHOULD HAVE TOLD YOU WHAT WAS WRONG WITH ME.

BUT MOM AND DAD WEREN'T TELLING ANYONE EXCEPT FAMILY, SO I . . . HOW COME YOU STOPPED BEING MY FRIEND?

. . . I DON'T KNOW.

I MEAN, ACTUALLY, I THINK I **DO** KNOW--THIS IS GOING TO SOUND RIDICULOUS, BUT I WAS JEALOUS.

WHAT?! JEALOUS OF ME? YOU **WANTED** TO BE SICK?!

OF COURSE NOT. BUT, YOU WERE GETTING SO MUCH ATTENTION FROM THE TEACHERS. . . .

EVERYONE WAS ALWAYS ASKING YOU HOW YOU FELT, AND GIVING YOU EXTENSIONS ON OUR ASSIGNMENTS. . . .

AND YOU GOT TO MISS A TON OF SCHOOL.

LAINE, I MISSED SO MUCH I NEARLY HAD TO **REPEAT** SIXTH GRADE.

ARE YOU SERIOUS? WOW. I DIDN'T KNOW THAT. WELL, ANYWAY, REMEMBER BOBBY REEDER?

HE THOUGHT YOU WERE CONTAGIOUS, AND FOR SOME REASON, I BELIEVED HIM. SINCE I WAS YOUR BEST FRIEND, I WAS POSITIVE I WAS GOING TO GET "IT," WHATEVER IT WAS.

OH.

WHEN MY PARENTS FOUND OUT ABOUT OUR FIGHT, THEY WERE PRETTY MAD AT ME. WE TALKED ABOUT IT, BUT I DIDN'T KNOW HOW TO APOLOGIZE TO YOU.

THAT'S WHY I NEVER WROTE TO YOU AFTER YOU MOVED AWAY.

WELL, I **WAS** PRETTY MAD. . .

127

BUT I GUESS IT WOULD'VE HELPED IF I'D TOLD YOU THE TRUTH.

Poke!

YOU KNOW, EVERY NOW AND THEN, I WONDER ABOUT THE PEOPLE HERE.

LIKE WHO?

WELL, I REMEMBER DEIRDRE DUNLOP USED TO BRAG SHE'D BE THE FIRST IN OUR CLASS TO OUTGROW HER TRAINING BRA.... DID SHE?

SNORT!

YES! AND THE **DAY** SHE CAME IN WEARING HER NEW BRA, LOWELL JOHNSTON ASKED HER FOR A DATE!

NO WAY!

POP CORN

POP CORN

STACEY, LOOK!

THE MOVIE'S OVER?! WOW! WE MISSED THE WHOLE THING!

YEAH!

BUT IT WAS WORTH IT!

LAINE AND I REALIZED WE HAD A LOT OF CATCHING UP TO DO, SO WE MADE THE MOST OF THE WEEKEND.

AND WHEN WE WENT TO SLEEP ON SUNDAY NIGHT, I FELT LIKE A HUGE WEIGHT HAD BEEN LIFTED FROM MY CHEST.

'NIGHT, LAINE.

'NIGHT, STACE.

WELL, TWO, ACTUALLY...

HELLO, DR. BARNES... YES, I'M SORRY, BUT WE'VE DECIDED TO CANCEL THE REST OF STACEY'S TESTS THIS WEEK.

AND THEN WE WERE **HOME!!**

LATER THAT AFTERNOON...

STACEY, YOU ARE HOME EARLY! EVERYTHING IS ALL RIGHT, I HOPE?

YES, FINE, MIMI! IS CLAUDIA UPSTAIRS?

OF COURSE!

STACE!!

HI, CLAUD!

OH, WE MISSED YOU SO MUCH! WHAT A CRAZY WEEKEND, I HAVE SO MUCH TO TELL YOU....

JAMIE AND CHARLOTTE AND THE OTHER KIDS TOLD THEIR PARENTS **EVERYTHING**. YOU SHOULD HAVE SEEN LIZ'S AND MICHELLE'S FACES TODAY DURING... WAIT, HOW WAS NEW YORK?

IT WAS GOOD. REALLY, REALLY GOOD. BUT TELL ME MORE ABOUT WHAT HAPPENED!

WELL, WE SHOULD PROBABLY WAIT UNTIL KRISTY AND MARY ANNE GET HERE BEFORE--

I'LL GET IT!

RING!

BABY-SITTERS CLUB. HI, MRS. NEWTON!

HELLO, STACEY!

I'VE GOT A MEETING OF THE LITERARY CIRCLE AT MY HOUSE ON FRIDAY AFTERNOON, AND I NEED SOMEONE TO WATCH LUCY AND KEEP JAMIE BUSY FOR A COUPLE OF HOURS.

OH, I'LL DO IT! WHAT TIME?

3:00.

OH, AND I THOUGHT YOU'D LIKE TO KNOW . . .

I HAD A TALK WITH CATHY MORRIS. I THINK SHE HONESTLY DIDN'T REALIZE WHAT SHE'D DONE WRONG.

I ALSO CALLED THE JOHANSSENS, THE PIKES, THE GIANMARCOS, THE DODSONS. . . . IT TURNS OUT JAMIE AND CHARLOTTE WEREN'T THE ONLY UNHAPPY CHILDREN.

I WANT YOU TO KNOW HOW GRATEFUL WE ARE THAT YOU GIRLS WERE BRAVE ENOUGH TO TELL US WHAT WAS GOING ON.

STACEY, YOU **KNOW** YOU'RE SUPPOSED TO OFFER EVERY JOB THAT COMES ALONG TO ALL THE MEMBERS OF THE CLUB.

I'M SORRY.... I JUST FORGOT. I WAS SO EXCITED.

...I KNOW.

IT'S OKAY, I'D BE PRETTY EXCITED ABOUT SITTING FOR LUCY, TOO. BESIDES...I'VE BROKEN THAT RULE OFTEN ENOUGH MYSELF.

STACEY!

CHAPTER 15

THE PHONE RANG ALL THAT AFTERNOON. AT 6:00, WE WERE FEELING MUCH BETTER ABOUT OURSELVES.

I WONDER IF ANYONE WILL CALL US TONIGHT, WHEN WE'RE AT HOME!

PROBABLY.

WITH CHRISTMAS SO CLOSE, EVERYBODY IS GOING TO PARTIES, DINNERS, CONCERTS . . .

THIS MAY BE OUR BUSIEST SEASON YET!

DO YOU GUYS THINK THE BABY-SITTERS AGENCY WILL GET ANY MORE CALLS?

I **REALLY** DOUBT IT.

135

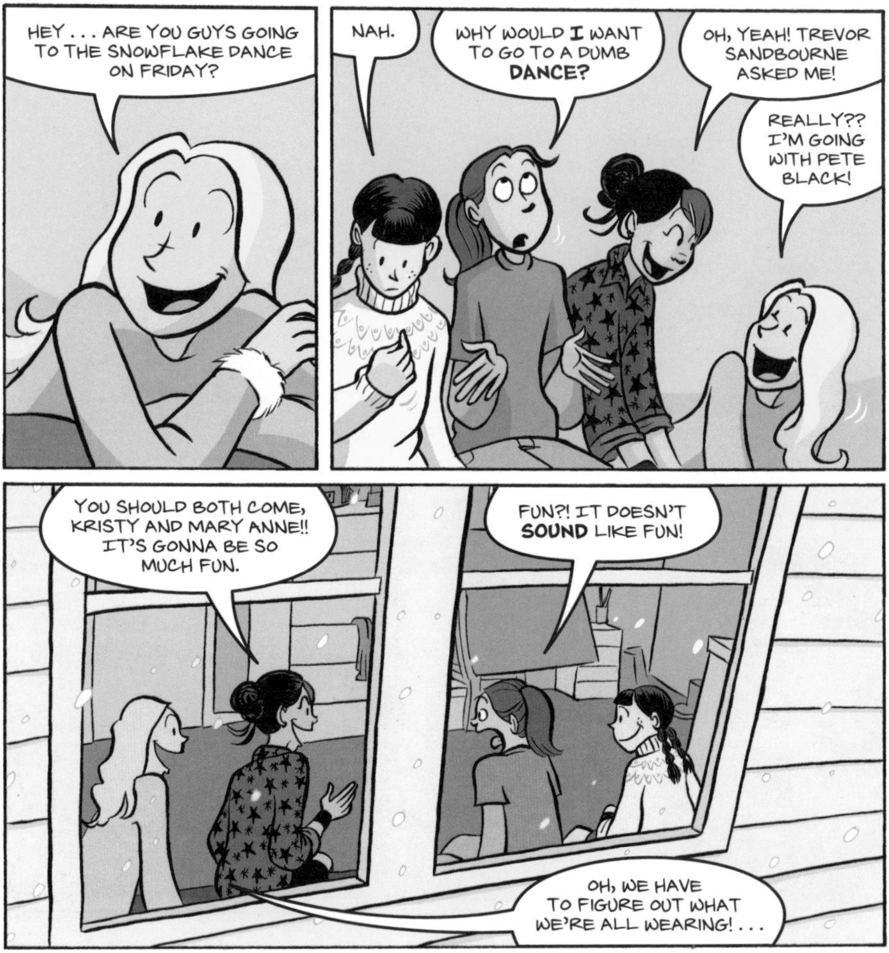
HEY . . . ARE YOU GUYS GOING TO THE SNOWFLAKE DANCE ON FRIDAY?
NAH.
WHY WOULD I WANT TO GO TO A DUMB DANCE?
OH, YEAH! TREVOR SANDBOURNE ASKED ME!
REALLY?? I'M GOING WITH PETE BLACK!
YOU SHOULD BOTH COME, KRISTY AND MARY ANNE!! IT'S GONNA BE SO MUCH FUN.
FUN?! IT DOESN'T SOUND LIKE FUN!
OH, WE HAVE TO FIGURE OUT WHAT WE'RE ALL WEARING! . . .

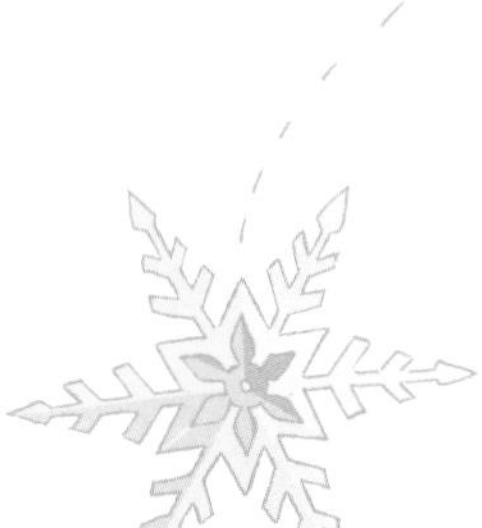

A WEEK LATER...

RING!

HELLO?

STACEY?

LAINE! HI!

WHAT'S HAPPENING WITH YOUR BABY-SITTING CLUB? LAST WEEKEND YOU SAID SOMETHING ABOUT SOME AGENCY?

OH MY GOSH, YOU'LL NEVER BELIEVE IT...

ALL OF OUR CLIENTS STOPPED CALLING THE BABY-SITTERS AGENCY BECAUSE THEY COULDN'T TRUST THE MEMBERS! AND THEN WHEN WE GOT TO SCHOOL ON TUESDAY...

YEAH?

. . . LIZ AND MICHELLE WERE HANDING OUT FLIERS FOR A **NEW** BUSINESS!!

MAKEOVERS, INC.?

YOU PAY THEM $5.00, AND THEY SHOW YOU HOW TO PUT ON MAKEUP, FIGURE OUT THE BEST WAY FOR YOU TO FIX YOUR HAIR . . .

OH, NO THANKS.

NOBODY SEEMED INTERESTED IN THEIR NEW SCHEME!

HA HA!

OH, AND GUESS WHAT-- CHARLOTTE JOHANSSEN, THE LITTLE GIRL WHO WAS HAVING TROUBLE WITH HER CLASSMATES...

YEAH?

HER TEACHER IS GOING TO SKIP HER INTO **THIRD** GRADE! THE WORK IN SECOND GRADE IS TOO EASY FOR HER.

THAT'S WHY THE OTHER KIDS WERE TEASING HER.

CHARLOTTE'S REALLY EXCITED ABOUT STARTING FRESH IN THE NEW YEAR.

AWW. THAT'S GOOD ... I REALLY WISH I COULD MEET HER--I'D LOVE TO MEET **ALL** YOUR FRIENDS THERE, STACEY.

WELL, YOU SHOULD COME VISIT ME IN STONEYBROOK!

REALLY??

YES! AND WHEN YOU DO...

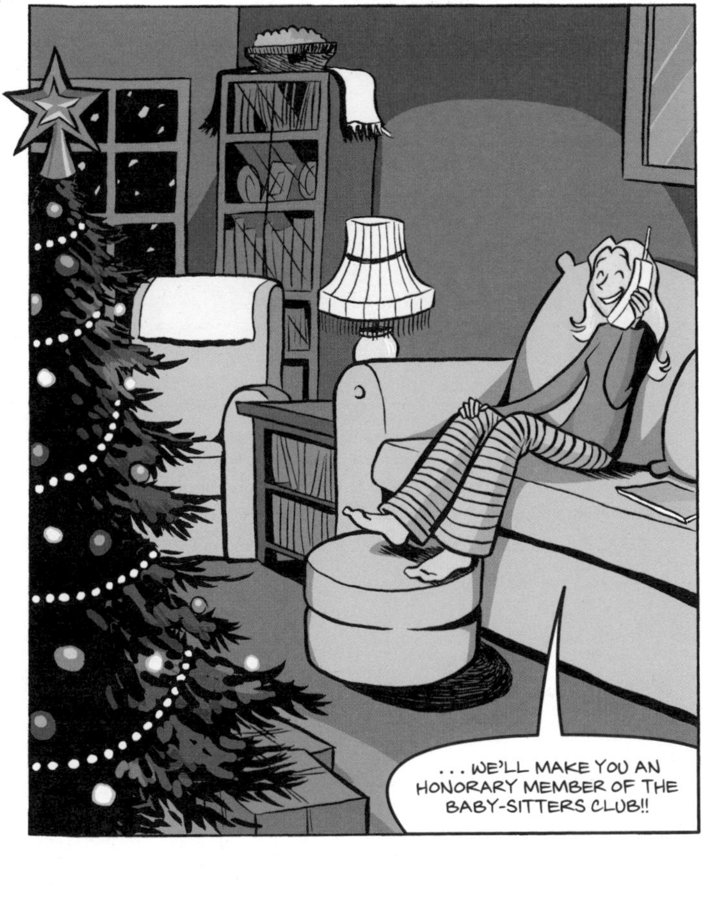
. . . WE'LL MAKE YOU AN HONORARY MEMBER OF THE BABY-SITTERS CLUB!!

This book is for my old pal, Claudia Werner
A. M. M.

Thanks to Marion Vitus, Adam Girardet, Duane Ballanger,
Lisa Jonte, Arthur Levine, and Braden Lamb. As always, a huge
thank-you to my family, my friends, and especially, Dave.
R. T.

Library of Congress Control Number: 2014945627

ISBN 978-0-545-81388-4 (hardcover)
ISBN 978-0-545-81389-1 (paperback)

10 9 8 7 6 5 4 3   16 17 18 19

Printed in the U.S.A.   88
First color edition printing, August 2015

Lettering by John Green
Edited by David Levithan, Janna Morishima, and Cassandra Pelham
Book design by Phil Falco
Creative Director: David Saylor